THE WHITE COCKADE.

ALSO BY RAY GRANT TOEPFER

The Scarlet Guidon

THE
WHITE
COCKADE

by Ray Grant Toepfer

CHILTON BOOKS

A Division of Chilton Company
Publishers
Philadelphia and New York

PUBLISHED IN PHILADELPHIA
BY CHILTON COMPANY
AND SIMULTANEOUSLY IN TORONTO,
CANADA, BY AMBASSADOR BOOKS, LTD.

LIBRARY OF CONGRESS CATALOG CARD
NUMBER 66-12910
DESIGNED BY ELIZABETH SURBECK

MANUFACTURED IN THE UNITED STATES
OF AMERICA

To my mother
and
to the memory of my father

THE WHITE COCKADE

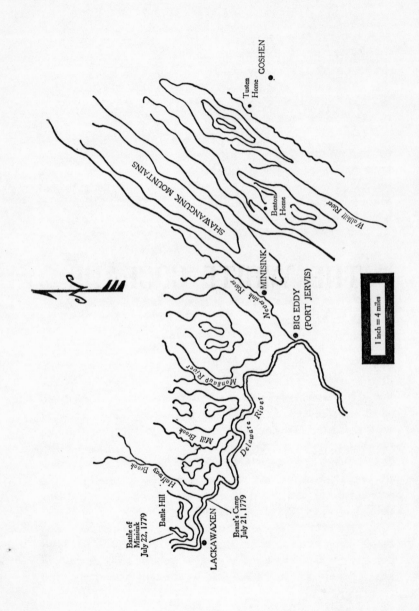

GOSHEN

Tusten
Home

Benton
Home

Wallkill River

SHAWANGUNK MOUNTAINS

Neversink River

MINISINK

BIG EDDY
(PORT JERVIS)

Mongaup River

Mill Brook

Delaware River

Holbrook Brook

Battle of
Minisink
July 22, 1779

Battle Hill

Brant's Camp
July 21, 1779

LACKAWAXEN

1 inch = 4 miles

ONE

JOEL BENTON was awakened by the sound of the wind keening down off the mountains to the west. He lay still for a moment, relishing the warmth of the bearskin that covered him, and then he looked towards the fireplace to see whether the fire was still alive beneath its blanket of ashes.

Reluctantly, he threw off the bearskin and pulled on his moccasins and his deerskin leggins, stiff with cold, and went over to the hearth. Beneath the ashes coals glowed softly orange. He fed small sticks into the fire from the pile beside the fireplace and blew upon the coals until the sticks caught. With a turkey wing he fanned them into a blaze until the heat spread out across the puncheon floor to meet him.

At fifteen and a half, Joel was already as tall as most men. He stood just under six feet and he weighed one hundred and forty pounds, as nearly as he could judge by the scales at Jonas' store down in Minisink village. A boyhood spent on the New York frontier had given him a graceful, wiry strength. He could track game, find his way through unfamiliar woods at night, and make a fire with damp wood. It had stood him in good stead when his father had become ill, because hunting and farming had been thrust upon him suddenly. He was thankful now that he had been strong enough to accept the responsibility.

He combed his wiry black hair with the hand-whittled maple comb he kept in his hunting bag and then he scrubbed his teeth with the frayed end of a spruce twig dipped in salt. There wasn't much salt left, he thought regretfully. And when it was gone, there would be no more. The Army needed all the salt it could get to preserve meat for the troops in the field.

Over on the other pallet his father coughed. A deep, rasping cough, low in the chest. His father had taken sick the winter before, shortly after his mother had died, and the cough had lingered through the summer, consuming him with its intensity, leaving him gasping for breath after each attack.

"Pa? Are you all right?"

His father stared at him while he struggled to contain the coughing. Finally he succeeded. He even managed a grin. "I'm finer than frog's hair, son. If you don't listen to the noise."

He forced himself to grin back. "I can stand it, Pa."

"How's the wood supply?"

"Pretty good. I've got enough cut for the next month and there's enough inside to last through the day."

"That's fine. It's going to be cold today."

"I know. I heard the wind."

His father nodded. "We're pretty near halfway through November, so we can expect anything to happen, now."

"Well," Joel said practically. "There's one good thing. The colder it gets, the less chance there is of an Indian raid. Even the British can't get the Indians to raid this late in the year."

"That's so. Maybe you ought to go in to Minisink today and pick up what you need for the winter. If we get much snow, you may not be able to get out for a while."

"All right. We ought to have a couple of pounds of rifle powder and a pig of lead. I want to mold bullets whenever it's too cold to hunt or chop wood. Anything else?"

His father considered. "Well, we could always use some flour. And beans, if they have any. Maybe a jug of molasses, if you can get it."

Joel grinned. "I can try, but I don't hold out much

hope. They haven't had molasses down at Minisink since last year. Or was it seventy-six?"

"That's the worst of the British. I can be patriotic and drink sassafras tea and spruce beer and like it, but I hate to give up my molasses."

"We've got maple sugar."

"Don't like maple sugar." His father looked at him with pretended truculence. "I don't for a fact."

Joel chuckled. "I'll see what I can do," he promised. "I've got three good deerskins and two bushels of corn I can take in. That ought to buy us whatever they've got to sell."

"See if you can get some news of the war, too. That's the worst part of being cooped up like this. A man can't hear what's going on in the world."

Joel reached up and took the rifle off its pegs and went to the door. "I'll be back directly. I want to get some water from the creek."

Outside the sky was gray and lowering. The wind scoured the snow off the cornfield where the frozen stubble had caught it. Joel looked around carefully, watching the creek for the telltale movement of a lurking Indian. Then he made a quick circuit of the cabin, keeping well away from the walls. In the gray light of early dawn he could see nothing but the solid crust of old snow, broken only by his own footprints. It was safe to go for water.

The surface of the little creek was frozen, but there was a soft spot at the outside of a bend where the ice was never too thick to be chopped out. This morning he was able to pound a hole in the ice with a sharp rock. He wondered whether that meant that he would have to ford the creek and its tributary on his way to Minisink. He would do better waiting for a hard freeze, if that were the case. When he had filled his pail, he walked upstream on the ice and then he turned towards the west, towards Minisink, and walked carefully forward. The ice creaked, but it held. He would be able to cross dry-shod.

3

When he got back to the cabin, his father was already up and dressed. He was stirring mush in the cooking pot over the fire with a long, hand-whittled wooden spoon.

"Come and get it, son. It's just what the doctor ordered."

Joel set the water bucket on the floor near the hearth, where it would not freeze during the day. "Speaking of doctors," he said, "why don't I take a run over to Goshen instead? I could get the doctor from there to come out and take a look at you."

His father shook his head stubbornly. "Nonsense. A good herb drench once a day for the next week and you doctoring me and I'll be fit as a fiddle. Especially if you get some molasses."

Joel knew that there was no point in arguing with his father. There were some things which Caleb Benton believed in with the whole of his being. One of them was that he could treat his illness as efficiently as could any doctor.

"I wish you could have had more schooling," his father said abruptly. "Not just what your mother and I were able to give you. It would have been a fine thing if you could have been a doctor or a lawyer or something like that."

"Maybe I can still," Joel said. "Once we get more land cleared and you get on your feet again, I could study at night."

"That's so." His father smiled tolerantly at him and suddenly he knew that his father was aware that he would not last through the winter, that the coughing, which had already resulted in bleeding, would only get worse until finally it would kill him.

They ate their mush in silence. It would have tasted better with a little salt, Joel thought. But salt was a scarce commodity, because of the war. If you worried at it long enough, you could blame the war for a lot of things. You could blame the war for the big house being burned down by a band of Tories leaving to serve the King. You could blame the war for Pa taking sick trying to scratch a living

4

for them out of the wilderness. You could blame the war for Mother's death of fever. Gentlewomen weren't made for the frontier, and the Delaware River Valley had once again become the frontier.

Although the Valley had been settled a hundred years ago, the Delaware Indians had continued to live there, until they had been driven out by the more warlike Iroquois tribes: the Mohawks, the Oneidas, the Onondagas, the Cayugas, and the Senecas. After a while, the whites had made peace with the Iroquois, and they had even fought side by side twenty years ago, in 1758, in the French and Indian War. But now things were different. The Onondaga claimed to be neutral, but that was doubtful. Only the Oneidas were friendly to the cause of the colonists. The rest of the tribes were actively on the side of the British, accompanying their armies and raiding parties down from Canada, burning and looting and killing.

It was not entirely the Indians' fault, Pa said. If the Continental Congress could only have acted quickly enough and wisely enough, the Indians would have been on the side of the colonists. But the Congress had sent out men who were unfriendly to the Indians, who refused or had no authority to promise them anything of value after the war. And the Indians had walked out of the council, never to return. That was why the Delaware Valley was the frontier again.

In 1775, the year the war began, the Valley had still been a safe place in which to live. The Revolutionary party had organized its supporters and those who still remained loyal to the King had also banded together, but there was no action, only talk. Even in the next year, it was safe, because those Tories who might have caused trouble moved out, preferring to live in New York City, where feeling was still strong for the King, or to remove to Canada, where there was no question of the Revolution spreading.

But last year, in 1777, Joseph Brant had led his Indians down from Niagara to a place called Oriskany Creek and ambushed a militia army under General Herkimer. Brant

5

was the Mohawk brother-in-law of Sir William Johnson, who had been forced to leave the Mohawk Valley by the patriots. In a sense, he had two axes to grind: one as a full-blooded Mohawk, and the other as a confirmed Tory. Joel could remember hearing the news of the battle three weeks later, in the store at Minisink. The usual band of loafers had been hanging around the store and they expressed sympathy for the settlers of the Mohawk Valley, who would have to bear the brunt of Johnson's wrath. The war was a long way off.

Two weeks later, a small army of Indians and Rangers swept down on the Delaware settlements. Minisink had barely escaped destruction, but several of the outlying houses had been burned and the wheat standing in the fields had been put to the torch.

Only this last July, another band of Rangers and Indians had raided south to Minisink again, causing the alarm to be sounded and driving isolated settlers into the relative safety of the small stockade which had been erected after the first raid.

The Rangers were under the command of Walter Butler, also a former inhabitant of the Mohawk Valley, and his son John, who had been an attorney for several years. They usually operated in conjunction with the Indian forces, which were under the direct control of Joseph Brant. Some people said that the Rangers were more to be feared than the Indians.

At first the settlers had been proud of the way they had stood off the raiders. No house had been burned, at least none near the stockade, and there had been no casualties. It was not until a week later that they discovered that the raid had merely been a diversion to conceal the fact that the main thrust was being made against the Wyoming Valley in Pennsylvania. If Brant had hit Minisink with his full force, the settlement probably would have been wiped out.

Recently, however, the Orange County militia had been placed under the command of a Doctor Tusten, who

6

lived in Goshen. He was the same doctor whom Joel had suggested going for earlier. It remained to be seen what unified command could accomplish.

Caleb Benton had been skeptical. "I don't see that a doctor has any special qualifications for leading men in battle," he said when he heard the news. "And if he's any good at that, then why is he a doctor?"

This morning, however, none of his father's irritation had been expressed. Joel's father was much too ill to worry about the qualifications required for battle leadership.

"Dress warmly," he told Joel, just as if he wasn't almost sixteen.

"I will, Pa." He still had a good woolen coat, saved from the burning of the house. With that underneath his deerskin hunting shirt, he would be as warm as toast, especially once he started moving along with his load.

He turned to go. "I ought to be back in about six hours. Don't worry about it if I'm late, though. If the west creek isn't frozen, I'll have to ford it and that'll take time."

"How about the rifle?"

"I'll leave it with you, Pa. I won't be able to carry it and carry the rest of the load, too. It ought to be safe enough, as far as Indians are concerned. They're all halfway back to Niagara, by now."

"Well, watch out for wolves."

"I will." He waved once and then he went outside to fix up his load. The corn was in sacks which had been saved from the flour purchases during the year. Joel wasn't sure what the price was these days; the last he had heard, corn was selling for six dollars Continental currency. If he took one sack, he might not be able to get everything he needed. On the other hand, if he took both sacks, leaving only the seed corn behind, he would have to stop to fix up a sled. The sacks weighed a good fifty pounds apiece. He might be able to carry one the eight miles into the village; he would never make it with two.

In the end, he decided not to make the sled, but to make two trips, instead. If the snow held off, he could go to town again tomorrow, and if it didn't he could probably hold out until the snow froze a good hard crust and he could use showshoes.

He carefully tied the sack in the deerskins to protect it, lashing the thongs securely so that they would not slip. Then he heaved the sack to his right shoulder, passed it around until it was centered, and grasped the thong ends in each hand.

At first the going was easy, down through the cornfield where the wind had swept the snow right down to the bare ground, and across the east fork of the creek. Then he began to climb the high ridge on the far side of the creek and the wind hit him like a blow. He stopped and looked back at the house. The logs were a rough, dirty gray against the snow, as if someone had tried to draw a picture of it with a sharpened bullet. He could make out the detail of the notched corners, the individual stones in the chimney, even the wisp of gray smoke torn all ragged by the wind. He turned away with satisfaction. Unless you stood on this ridge or the one next to it, you wouldn't be able to see the house. Not in this weather.

Until he reached the west branch of the creek, he stuck to the ridges. The wind had cleaned the snow away pretty well and it made easier going than the valleys, which were bound to be drifted deep.

When he crossed the west branch, he put the bundle down on a log and stopped for a breather. The west branch meant that he was halfway there. Now there was a steep climb for maybe a mile and a half and then a mile of steep downhill. Then there would be two miles of gently rolling land, usually planted in wheat, and then he would come to the settlement.

8

It was a good thing he had stuffed his moccasins with dried moss, he decided. It was about the only way to keep your feet from freezing. It was good that it was cold, too; his feet were staying dry. It was easy to get sore feet walking in wet moccasins.

By the time he got over the big rise and started on the downhill part, he was feeling the ache in his shoulders. It was hard going and no mistake, but he felt a stubborn sort of pride in his ability to carry the sack. Not many boys going on sixteen could carry a sack of corn eight miles, he thought. He was glad that he was big for his age.

It was blowing so hard now that he couldn't see the outline of the settlement, as he would have been able to do on a clear day. He stopped when he got to the edge of the flat lands and checked his bearings as best he could from the notch on the ridge behind him. He was a little south of Minisink, now; he had let the wind head him off some, he guessed. He put the sack down and shrugged his shoulders to get the blood moving in them again.

In front of him, half obliterated by the wind, the tracks of a deer showed plainly. The deer had probably come by within the last couple of hours, or the tracks wouldn't be visible at all. It was a funny thing for a deer to come out across the open fields in daylight. He thought about it for a minute. The deer had to be scared to come out in the open that way. For a minute he thought about Indians, but then he discarded the notion. Even an Indian had to have shelter and food. Where was he going to find either in hostile country at this time of year? No. The deer had probably been scared by a catamount or by a farmer on his way into town.

Joel picked up his sack and settled it on his shoulders. The next time I put you down, he told the sack, it's going to be in Jonas' store, where it's good and warm.

TWO

HEAT swelled from the big fireplace at the back end of the store when Joel entered. Jim Hickey and Orin Cade were standing in front of it, arguing about the necessity for calling the militia out in winter. Jonas himself was tactfully taking no part in the discussion.

The store smelled pleasantly of spices, of cloth bolts, of tobacco and spirits; all compounded into an almost tangible odor of comfort, security, and well-being. Despite the ravages of three years of war, Jonas' shelves still held bolts of good English cloth, and an imposing array of tricorne hats, ladies' bonnets, and even a pair of black riding boots, topped with tan leather. Joel was not fooled by the apparent plenty. Since the war had interrupted the lucrative logging industry along the Delaware, few people could afford to buy the expensive items in Jonas' store. That was why they were still there. The cheaper, more practical goods had been sold long ago.

Joel closed the door behind him and let the bundle slide down from his shoulders.

"Well, bub," Jonas greeted him. "Looks like you got you quite a load there."

Jonas was a small, wiry man with a cast in his right eye. You could never be sure with which eye Jonas was watching you. The children of the village had a joke to the effect that Jonas could do his bookkeeping with one eye and watch the store with the other.

"The load didn't get any lighter," Joel admitted. "Morning, Mr. Hickey, Mr. Cade."

11

The two men at the fireplace interrupted their argument long enough to say hello and then they went back to it.

Jonas winked his right eye at Joel. "You'd think they'd get tired of chewing on an old bone, wouldn't you? Especially since there's nothing they can do about it anyhow."

"I don't know. What's it all about?"

"Well, the colonel over to Goshen sent word out that the next time the Indians come out the militia is going after them. He says it ain't enough just to get inside the fort and let them burn everything outside. If we chase them, maybe they'll stay away."

"Sounds like it might be a good thing to do," Joel admitted.

"The only trouble is, nobody wants to leave his house and his family to go off chasing Indians. There's no guarantee that he'd find either one when he come back."

"I suppose not. The only thing is, though, somebody has to take the first step."

Jonas nodded. "That's the point. Who's going to do it? It's got to be somebody who doesn't have anything left to lose. As long as the Congress won't send regular troops out to defend the Valley, we're going to have raids. And their army needs our grain and cattle. It ain't only us that's hurting, Joel. It's them, too."

Joel thought about it for a moment. It was all right to say that the militia had to go out when you didn't have to go. But suppose you did have to go? He would join the militia himself, next birthday. What if he had to go and leave Pa alone in the cabin? Who would take care of Pa and hunt for him and take care of things? In winter he would need wood to keep warm. Who would chop his wood?

"It's a problem," he admitted finally.

Jonas nodded sagely and then, as if he had been reading Joel's mind, he asked how his father was doing.

12

"He's cheerful, but he's mighty sick," Joel told him.

Jonas nodded again. "Caleb never was one to make a poor mouth over things he couldn't help. I can't help thinking though that he ought to let that doctor come and take a look at him."

"I know it. The only thing is, he won't do it and I can't make him."

"I know. He always was stubborn as a mule." Jonas changed the subject. "What you got in there?"

"A bushel of Indian corn. Three good deerskins."

"Corn," Jonas said. "By grannies, that's something we can always use. I can't pay you in money, though. Only Continental."

"That's all right. I came to get some things. Maybe we can work out a trade."

Jonas nodded happily. "Why, sure. Let's us figure it."

In the end, Joel decided that he had done pretty well. Jonas figured the corn to be worth six dollars and fifty cents Continental or five shillings King's money. The hides he figured at a dollar apiece. He told Joel that it would take care of the lead and the powder and the sack of flour.

"The thing is, I don't have no rifle powder. Only the coarse kind for muskets. But what you can do is grind it finer yourself. You take two pieces of wood and you go real slow. You know how?"

Joel said that he knew how. If you took a little at a time, it wasn't too dangerous. And in any case, they needed the powder. Generally, when you had to do something badly enough, you found a way to do it.

"Now the molasses," Jonas said. "That there is a horse of a different color. I had a keg in October and it run out. I can't get no more."

"Pa will be sorry to hear that. He has a sweet tooth."

Jonas thought about it. "How are you going to carry this stuff back?"

13

"Hadn't given it much thought. I figured the powder and lead could go inside my shirt and the sack and jug could kind of hang on behind."

"Tell you what," Jonas said. "Since you can't get the molasses, you can have one of them hides to wrap it up in so your flour won't get wet. I'll figure that it still comes out even. And if you wait a minute, I got me an idea."

Jonas disappeared into the storeroom in back. Jim Hickey turned from the fire and said to no one in particular that he guessed it was about time he was getting home. Orin Cade grinned at Joel as if to say he had gotten the best of the argument.

"See anything exciting when you come down, Joel?" he asked.

"Nothing but wind and snow." And then he remembered. "There were deer tracks out in the wheatfields. Fresh ones. I figure they were made maybe an hour before I came by."

Orin nodded. "Sometimes they cut across there. It's not too often they come out of the woods in daylight, though."

"I know it."

"Well," Orin said. "It must have been a catamount or wolves scared that deer. It's too consarned cold for Indians. You take an Indian, he's got better sense than to go running around the woods when he can sit in a nice warm birch house."

Jonas emerged from the dark storeroom triumphantly carrying what seemed to be a pig's bladder. "Here," he said. "I pulled the bung out and scraped around with an old spoon. There's probably some splinters, but it's the best I could do."

The pungent odor of molasses permeated the room. It smelled fine, like rum and taffy and spice, all together.

"Mighty nice of you," Joel said.

Jonas spread his hands expressively. "It's just to sweeten the trade, you might say."

"Well, thanks. Pa will surely be pleased."

14

Jonas nodded. "You give him my regards, will you? Tell him I hope he can get in himself, next time."

The load was a good deal lighter on the way back, Joel thought ruefully. In some ways they would have done better to keep back half of the corn and do without the flour, but then they couldn't have gotten the lead, or at least not as much of it. It was probably better the way it was. You couldn't live on corn all the time. You had to have meat, and meat meant hunting.

He made good time on the long uphill grade from Minisink, because the wind was at his back now, pushing him right along. Once he got through the notch in the ridge he was protected from the wind and so it couldn't help him, either, but it was downhill going until he came to the west fork of the creek.

After he got up that rise, he decided that it was about time to stop for a rest. It would have been nice if he could have made it home without stopping, just to show that he could do it, but the load was getting so that it was wearing him down. He picked a spot where an overhanging rock came near to the trail and then he cut off and put the bundle down and sat back out of the wind, letting the blood pump through his tired shoulders.

The wind was dying down now. You could still hear it in the high trees, but it was nowhere near as loud as it had been before. As he watched, he saw a flurry of snow dance past and then another. The sky was heavier than it had been, too.

He stood up. If it was going to start snowing, it was a good idea to get back to the house as soon as he could. It was a foolish man who let himself be caught in the woods without snowshoes and without a rifle.

He was mid-way up the last rise before the east branch of the creek when he heard the shots. First there was a sharp ringing one, a rifle. Then there was a flurry of dull booms from smooth-bore muskets. And then he heard the yelling. It

15

sounded like the sort of noise you might hear if a pack of wolves came on you suddenly on a dark night.

The rifle rang out again and suddenly he knew what it meant. He freed himself of the bundle and pitched it as far from him as he could, aiming at the low bushes near the big maple. That way the snow would cover it so that it would look like a rock. Then he began to run up the rise.

When he was almost at the top he fell to his hands and knees and crawled the rest of the way until he could see through the spiky brush at the crest.

At first he thought that nothing had happened yet, because the house was still standing and the Indians were milling around in the yard, but then the door burst open and two Indians came out into the yard. One of them was holding two guns. He went across the yard to where a man in a black cap and a green coat was standing, watching the scene. The man in the green coat reached out and took one of the guns and examined it. He reached in his pocket and gave something to the Indian who had given him the gun.

Just then, a puff of smoke eddied out through the doorway and then a yellow knife of flame pierced the bark roof and shot upwards. In a moment the entire roof was blazing, fanned by the wind, and suddenly the walls began to buckle inward.

It was as if there were two of him. One part of him wanted to run down through the yard full of Indians and smash his way through the burning walls to get to Pa. And the other part of him didn't want to move, didn't want to do anything at all, because there wasn't anything that anybody could do any more.

He tasted blood and suddenly he realized that he had bitten his hand until it bled and then he remembered that he had stuffed his hand into his mouth to keep from screaming or calling out.

Easy, he told himself. There's nothing that can be done now. It's all over. All you can do is try to get out of here before they catch you. If you can make one of the settlements, maybe somebody will go with you to help track them down. That's the only thing left to do. Make them pay for what they've done.

The man in the green coat raised something shiny to his mouth and a moment later he turned around. Joel could make out the blurred outline of his face, although he was a good three hundred yards away. He was a white man, probably one of Butler's Rangers in command of the raiding party. One officer and ten Indians. Not much of a raiding party. Were there others in the vicinity?

Three short whistle blasts sounded and the Indians came milling around the officer, who pointed northwest with the gun the Indian had given him. Something about the shape of the stock looked familiar and then it came to Joel. The gun was Pa's rifle.

He jerked abruptly and at that moment the officer turned and looked straight up the ridge. For a split-second he could see the man's face. It was too far away to make out individual features, but he could see the white cockade on the man's skullcap, the arrogant, hawklike thrust of the nose and chin. The man stiffened and Joel froze in place. Maybe he hadn't been seen. The officer was turning back to the Indians, just as if everything was normal. No. Two of them had left the group and were fading into the underbrush on the north side of the clearing. In a minute they would start working around the bend of the creek to cut him off.

He backed down the hill as quickly as he could until he judged it was safe to stand up and then he started to run. If they thought that he hadn't noticed them, they would move cautiously and that would take time. If he could get far enough ahead of them, perhaps the snow would cover his tracks and then he might be safe.

He raced down the first slope almost at top speed and his impetus carried him almost up the next rise before he had to put effort into it. He pounded away until he got just over the crest and then he slowed down to a trot. He stopped then to catch his breath and he remembered that he hadn't eaten anything since this morning. All told, it wasn't the way he would have chosen to make a run for his life. He had traveled close to fourteen miles so far, all of it under a heavy load. Now he had to run another seven miles.

He let the cold air come into his lungs until his head cleared and then he turned around to look at his back trail. The snow was still falling, but his tracks were plain, even the tracks he had made on the way home from Minisink. The tracks he had made in the morning were gone, of course; that was probably the only thing that had saved him. If they had seen his first set of tracks, they would have been waiting for him in the woods.

He looked back at the rise near the creek and then he saw the Indians. There were three of them, now, and they had come in from two sides, hoping that he would still be there waiting and watching the clearing. Now they were milling around looking at his tracks, trying to decide how much of a start he had on them, he supposed.

He began to trot down the hill.

By the time Joel reached the west branch of the creek, his breath was coming more easily. He had hit his second wind and he knew then that he could keep up the easy lope he had chosen for the next couple of hours, if he had to. The only thing wrong with that was that once they found his tracks they would try to run him down. First one would sprint and then another and he would have to run at top speed constantly until he collapsed. The only thing to do was to keep at the lope as long as he could and hope that he would hit the long downslope before they caught him. He could outrun them on that. And maybe, if he was lucky, the snow would cover his tracks.

He started up the long, steep climb and when he reached a clear spot he looked behind him.

They were doing just what he had expected. Two of them were trotting along at an even, wind-saving pace, and the third was sprinting down to the creek. Terror seized him as he realized how fast they must have come. There was no longer the ghost of a chance that the snow would erase his tracks in time for him to evade them. He ran across the clear ground with his breath coming in short, shallow gasps, and then a musket boomed behind him. He heard the drone of the ball and then the thud as it struck a tree far to the right. One of the two in the rear must have fired and they were a good three hundred yards away. You had to be lucky to hit anything with a smoothbore at three hundred yards. He didn't have to worry too much about that. The thing he had to worry about was the man in front who would try to get close enough to get a shot at close range, say a hundred yards or less. Or maybe he would try to get even closer and throw his tomahawk. That could be a good deal more dangerous. Again fear grasped him and squeezed the breath from his chest.

Stop it, he commanded himself. If you get scared enough, you'll just quit running and let them catch you. All you have to do to get away from them now is keep ahead of the front one on this uphill stretch, where he's got everything in his favor. Once he wears himself out on that, he won't be able to catch you on the downhill. But you have to breathe. Breathe deeply. Suck it in, all the air you can get.

He kept one leaden foot moving ahead of the other and bent low to catch at rocks or roots to help him in the last scramble before he reached the top.

Two muskets boomed, one after the other. This time, he heard the balls come close, like angry bees. Either their shooting was improving or else they had narrowed the gap. Either way, it wasn't good.

19

As he saw the sky over the top of the ridge, he deliberately slackened pace for a moment and sucked in all the air he could. It felt fine, the clean, cold air and the sky ahead and then he was over the top and it was fine running after that on the last, long downhill grade to the wheatfields.

He let his legs stretch out to full stride, carrying himself tall, letting his chest swell with wind and then the leaden feeling left his feet and the terror uncoiled from his chest. One way or another, he was going to do it. He was going to outrun them.

When he got to the end of the long downslope he shot another look behind him. One Indian must have quit because there were only two of them now. They were coming down the slope fast, but no faster than he was. One of them held two muskets and he guessed that the other one had been chosen to make the last sprint in an effort to cut him off before he could reach the settlement.

As he watched, the one without the muskets began to push for the sprint. His legs moved quickly in the short, choppy steps a runner uses to get up speed. Joel faced front again. It wouldn't do to miss his footing on an icy spot now. He opened his stride up to the long, easy running step he needed for distance. He still had better than a mile and a half to go before anyone could help him. He deliberately held the pace, allowing the Indians to close the distance little by little, but when he risked another look behind him, he saw that they were less than two hundred yards behind him, driving hard, and then he knew that it was now or not at all. He put on a last burst of speed.

He called up all of his strength and he could feel the wind against his face as his speed increased. Now he was running over the hard stubble of the wheatfield and he could see the outline of the first house gray in the snow. Suddenly there were other houses ahead and he could even see the bulk of the stockade.

A musket boomed behind him and a moment later

he felt the ball hit his right arm and he faltered in his stride. It was like getting hit with the edge of a board. It hurt, but not so that you couldn't stand it. It had been lucky that his arm had been hit and not his leg. He could still manage to run. Another thing, the musket had had a sort of faraway sound. Maybe they weren't so close any more. He passed the first house and suddenly the door opened and he saw a man standing waiting for him to slow down and talk.

"Indians!" he croaked. The man reached over the door, probably for his gun, and then suddenly Joel plunged forward into darkness.

THREE

HE was warm and although he could not see the fire, he could feel it near him and he hoped that Pa was warm, too. He opened his eyes to look and then he saw that there were men standing around him, Jonas and Jim Hickey and Orin Cade and another man wearing a blue broadcloth coat and high black boots. He was in Jonas's store, lying on the big counter.

And then he remembered.

Pa was dead. The house was burned and the Indians were out. He thought about Pa waiting for him to come back, needing him, and about how he had been gone when Pa had needed him. He fought back tears.

"Easy, bub," Jonas said kindly, watching him with his right eye. "What happened?"

He looked at them and then he tried to push himself up. His right arm gave way immediately and then he managed to get up with his left arm alone and he looked at the neat bandage on his right arm.

"I got shot," he said. "They shot me."

"Who shot you?" the man in the broadcloth coat asked.

Now Joel could see the man's face, a pleasant sort of face with a tanned complexion that testified to an active, outdoor life, and regular habits. The blue eyes had laughter-crinkles running from the corners. The man's somewhat wavy brown hair was tied in a queue with a bit of scarlet ribbon.

"Indians. What tribe were they from?" the man asked.

"I couldn't tell. I got the idea that they were Mohawks, but I couldn't tell for sure."

Jonas broke in. "This here is Doctor Tusten, Joel. He's the colonel of the militia over to Goshen. He's got to know all about it so we can figure out what to do."

Joel nodded gravely. It was kind of important when a real live colonel was asking you about something you knew and he didn't.

"Well, I left here," he said. "I made pretty good time on the way back home. Just before I got to the last ridge I heard shots, so I threw my bundle under a tree and went up to the crest on all fours. There were about ten or twelve Indians and a white man in uniform. It looked like the kind Butler's Rangers wore last year when they raided down here. The uniform, I mean. It was all over by the time I got to the top of the ridge. Two of them came out of the house with Pa's rifle and then the house caught fire and burned. It burned awful fast. Then the officer—the one in uniform—blew a whistle to get them to move out. The only thing was, I moved just then and I guess he saw me, because he sent some of them out to chase me. At first, there were three of them, but then there were only two and I pretty near made it, only I kind of folded up at the end."

Doctor Tusten nodded. "You must have been exhausted. You fell and struck your head. That's why you've been unconscious for so long."

"How is my arm, sir?"

"It's going to be painful for a while, that's all. The ball missed the bone and went into the muscle. It didn't go in deep. I got it right out without a bit of trouble."

Hickey drew himself up to his full five-foot-three. "We'd better send out a party to trail them," he said. "How about it, Colonel?"

The doctor thought for a moment. "It won't do much good, Jim. They've had a good three hours head start on us and its still snowing. By the time we got back to this boy's

24

cabin to pick up the trail of the main party it would be gone."

"How about the two who chased him?"

"You can try if you like, but I don't think it'll do much good. A small party like that would probably split up and rendezvous some place further on. The only thing to worry about now is whether they're on their own or whether they're part of a larger group."

"That's so," Jonas said. "We rang the church bell and got everybody in the stockade just as soon as we knew. If there's more of them, we want to be ready."

"That's good," the doctor replied. "In the morning, send out a good-sized patrol, maybe twenty men, and scout around the town for three or four miles to see if you can pick up any tracks. You want to make sure they're not lurking in the woods. Meanwhile, I'll get back to Goshen and see what I can do about organizing a hunting party. We can spare the men better than you can, and if they're headed north, we'll have a chance of picking up a fresher trail."

Joel watched the doctor as he talked. He knew what he wanted to do and he went ahead and did it. That was something you could always admire in a man. But the best part of it was that he wasn't loud or angry or anything like that. He was calm and friendly and reasonable. Except for his clothes, which were obviously costly, there would have been nothing outstanding about him. But there was a certain undefinable something that made the others listen to him, treat him with respect and even with affection.

The doctor passed a big, capable-looking hand over his brown hair. "It's good and warm in here," he said approvingly. "I wish I could stay longer."

"Any time, and welcome," Jonas grinned. "I could even manage a drink of rum."

Doctor Tusten smiled. "I couldn't take that, Jonas. I might never want to leave." He turned back to Joel. "What do you think about the raid?"

25

"I think that this was a small party that got left behind or sent out by a bigger party. A group that small wouldn't be this far from Canada at this time of year. They'd have to get food and supplies and they're too few to attack a regular settlement where they could find them."

"What do you think they'll do now?" The question was as direct as a bullet. For all his easy-going manner, the doctor was no fool. He was thinking ahead every minute of the time.

"I think they just happened to come on the house. I think they were on their way to join up with a bigger band and start back for Canada and I think that that's what they've done. The bigger band is probably north of here, maybe way up near the Mohawk."

"Why would a little band like this come so far south?" Hickey asked.

Joel thought about it for a moment. "Maybe they were supposed to show themselves once or twice to scare people so the big band would have a chance to hit a bigger place without having to worry about the combined militia coming down on them."

"I don't know," Hickey said dubiously. "It seems like an awful lot of trouble to go to just for the sake of surprise."

"Never underestimate your opponent, Jim," the doctor said drily. "Bear in mind that Butler's no fool—neither the father nor the son. No matter how crazy it may sound to us, there's a good reason for it somewhere. This boy seems to have a good answer for it."

"But in the middle of winter?" Jonas broke in with a look of bewilderment.

"Butler's men and the Indians can survive where we can't. They can live off the country, even in winter. Some of these Indians can run through the woods eighty miles a day for a week on end with nothing more than a little sack of parched corn to eat. There's another thing. We've all got families to worry about. Butler's men are the Tories who were chased out of the Mohawk Valley and maybe even some

26

who were chased out of here. Their families are up in Canada now. Their homes are either burned to the ground or taken over by our people. They've got nothing left to lose but their lives."

"You really think they're raiding some place big?" Jim Hickey asked dubiously.

"I do," the doctor replied. "I'm going to get back over to Goshen and send a company out to see what they can find. The sooner we know where they're going to strike, the better off we'll be."

Joel slid off the counter and shook himself. His head ached dully and his arm throbbed, but otherwise he felt fine.

"Are you going to try to catch them, Colonel?" he asked.

"If we can pick up their trail in the morning."

"Can I go along?"

Doctor Tusten looked at him. "We'll be starting from Goshen," he said. "How would you get there and still be in condition to march through the woods all day?"

"I could ride over with you. If I had some place to sleep tonight, I'm sure I could make it."

"Now, Joel," Jonas said. "It's a cold night. Even the doctor here wouldn't have been out, if he hadn't had to see to Mrs. Thorpe."

Doctor Tusten looked at Joel.

"I can make it," Joel said. "When you catch up with them, I want to be there."

The doctor nodded. "All right. Jonas, can you lend this young man your horse? I can return it in the morning."

Jonas nodded. "Any time, Colonel."

As Jonas went out to saddle his horse, the doctor turned back to Joel. "Are you in the militia?" he wanted to know.

"Not yet, sir. I'm not sixteen."

The doctor nodded. "This is no time to be particular. If you want to join now, I'll see to it they let you in. Do you have any kinfolks?"

27

Joel shook his head. "Only my uncle Charley. He lives up in the Cherry Valley. We used to live up near there until the Tories burned us out and Pa came down here. He was a surveyor and he lost everything he had in the fire, except his rifle. He was sick even then, and he thought if we came further south the winters wouldn't be so cold and maybe he could get his strength back and start surveying again."

"I see." The doctor reached under his coat and drew forth a long, shiny pistol. "Can you use this if you have to?"

Joel nodded. "Yes, sir."

"Stick it in your belt, then. You may not need it, but it doesn't hurt to be ready."

The wind had died and the snow had all but stopped when they left the settlement, but the weather was much colder than it had been in the early afternoon. The horses' hooves creaked on the frozen crust as they rode along under the starshine.

The doctor had little to say. He remarked once that it was very cold. A little later he broke his silence again to say that they hadn't passed over any fresh trail.

Joel held his right arm close to his side to keep from joggling it. It wasn't broken, but it would take a while to heal. It was a good thing it hadn't been broken. It could have been a whole lot worse. He shivered suddenly, thinking of Pa alone in the cabin waiting for him, and then the moment of surprise, hearing the quick pad of running feet in time to fire the rifle and reload and fire again. And then there had been no more time.

He hoped that it had been quick for Pa, that he had been shot without being tortured. And then he remembered that he had heard nothing from the cabin, no yells or screams other than those the Indians had made. That was a lot to be thankful for.

Still and all, he had a funny feeling. He had never been alone before. When you came right down to it, there was nobody now except Uncle Charley and his new wife, whom Joel had never met. He couldn't claim kin with anyone else in the whole world. And as far as going to Uncle Charley for help, Uncle Charley probably had plenty of troubles of his own without taking on those of a boy who was almost a man. Well, if that was the way it had to be, there was nothing he could do about it except ride along. If he was supposed to be alone, then he'd make the best of it.

At that, he was starting out with more in life than a lot of people had. He wasn't bad-looking; he knew that from the way some of the girls in the settlement had stared at him and smiled whenever he came in to buy or trade with Jonas. He was taller than a lot of men; close to six feet, Pa used to tell him. He weighed a good hundred and forty pounds and Pa had taught him to fight and shoot and roam the woods before he had taken sick. Mother had taught him figures and how to read from the Bible and John Bunyan, even the hard words, and how to write a polite letter. He could hunt and trap and skin his meat. He could fix the lock of almost any rifle or musket he had ever seen. He could take a bullet out of a wound if he had to and tie the wound up so that it would heal clean besides. Somehow, somewhere, there had to be room for him.

Benjamin Tusten unsaddled the mare and turned her into her stall. When he turned back to the boy he found him struggling with the girths on Jonas's worn-out saddle.

"Better let me do that, Joel," he suggested quietly. "You don't want to strain that arm of yours."

"No, sir."

A quiet, obedient boy, the doctor decided. He wondered whether his eldest son, James, now almost nine, would be as well-mannered and self-reliant in six years. James was

29

on the wild side just now. But that was part of being a boy.

They walked up to the house together, the boy always a step or two behind him. Probably out of respect for my age, the doctor thought with some amusement. Well, he was thirty-six; there was no getting around it. When his father had been thirty-six he had thought that Father was getting to be an old man. It didn't seem so old now, but he could remember how it seemed to a fifteen-year-old boy.

Catherine and Susan were sitting in the kitchen by the fire when he opened the door.

"Ben! You're so late, dear!" Catherine said and then he saw her eyes widen as she saw Joel.

"My dear, this is Joel Benton. Joel, Mrs. Tusten. Susan, this is Joel. Joel, our niece Susan."

The boy bowed slightly. "Your servant, ma'am. Your servant, miss."

Courtly manners at that! The boy had been raised well. He didn't belong in a log house on the bank of a mountain creek.

"Joel has had a terrible experience, Catherine. His father was killed by Indians this afternoon, and Joel barely escaped with his life. He was pursued right up to the stockade. Perhaps we could fix him a bed in the corner of the kitchen?"

"Of course! Have either of you eaten?"

The doctor smiled. "I've had no supper, I'm afraid. And Joel can't have had anything all day. Is that right, Joel?"

"No, sir, I haven't. Not since—not since breakfast."

The doctor noticed Joel's hesitation. It was the last time he saw his father, he thought with quick intuition. But he's not going to cry in front of us.

"What about the Indians, Ben? Is there going to be another raid?"

"I don't think we're going to be raided," he told Catherine. "Captain Brown is supposed to come out tonight and

I'll give him orders to send out a patrol first thing in the morning. We'll give the early alarm meanwhile and that will have to do."

"Here's some hot stew, Uncle Ben," Susan said. She put down the plate and then she filled another one for the boy. She didn't say anything to him, but the doctor noticed that she smiled at him shyly.

"That smells good, Susan. You're getting to be quite a cook." He wondered whether Catherine had noticed the smile. Judging from the look of warm tolerance on her face, she had.

"What's the first alarm, sir?" the boy asked.

"Well, if there are Indians out in the general area, we ring the bell in the church steeple one time. That lets the people within hearing know that they'd better get ready in case they have to come to the stockade. If we've sighted the Indians, we ring the bell twice to let them know they have to start immediately. If we ring the bell three times, it means that we're under attack and that they'd better try to get to the stockade over at Minisink or take their chances in the strongest house they can find."

"That's what they do over at Minisink," Joel said. "Only we lived too far out to hear the bell and Pa was generally too sick to make the trip anyhow."

The boy ate almost automatically, as if the act were something he felt he had to perform, rather than one which he enjoyed. He's practically falling asleep over his plate, the doctor thought.

Susan disappeared for a moment and then returned with the straw-stuffed tick which they kept under the bed in the children's room for occasional visitors. "I brought the bed," she said shyly.

"Thank you, Susan," Catherine said. "Ben? Perhaps we'd better go in the parlor and let Joel get to sleep."

Joel smiled gratefully at her. "To tell the truth, ma'am, I am pretty tired."

While Susan and Catherine washed the dishes and

31

banked the fire, the doctor went into the parlor and lighted the wood that had been laid in the fireplace pending the arrival of company. When Captain Brown came, he would be cold. The captain would welcome a hot toddy. The doctor went back to the kitchen for the sugar bowl, the kettle, and a bottle of whiskey kept for the prevention of colds, the cure of snakebite—unless the patient died first—and other sundry ailments which responded to no other treatment. The whiskey didn't cure the ailments, but the patients usually felt better.

Catherine and Susan passed him in the hallway. When he opened the door, Joel was standing before the fire, looking into the flames that licked over the hickory log. He ran a hand over his face before he looked up.

"It's a mighty hot fire, sir," he said.

Doctor Tusten nodded gravely. "Hickory generally makes a hot fire."

He collected the sugar bowl and the whiskey and two glasses and put them on the table. Then he thought of something else.

"I'd like to mix you a hot toddy, Joel. Something to put you to sleep in a hurry."

The boy shook his head. "Thank you, sir. But it's not necessary. I can—fall asleep without it."

How was it, the doctor thought, that the young, who had so much more to lose, often showed the most courage when they had lost it?

He went over to the fire for the small kettle. And then he thought of something else.

"It sometimes seems as if a man is supposed to do the impossible, Joel. He hears that a man is supposed to keep a straight face, no matter what, and never show that he's hurt. It's a pack of lies. I never knew that it made a man any less of a man because he cried when something big happened to him."

"No, sir," Joel said gratefully.

"Goodnight," the doctor said as he closed the door behind him.

FOUR

THE Tustens were early risers, but even so Joel was up ahead of everybody else. He swept the ashes into the small shovel in the corner of the big fireplace and took them out to the ash-hopper just outside the back door to keep until the time for making soap. Then he went out to the well and brought in a pail of water. He couldn't handle much with his right hand, so he used his left. It was awkward at first, but then he got used to reaching for things with it and then it was almost as good as his right.

He had cried a little before he went to sleep. It was nothing to worry about, since the doctor had said it was all right. It was the way he felt, anyway. The thing was, he had felt a little guilty because he hadn't been with Pa when the Indians came. But he couldn't help not being there. And even if he had been there, he couldn't have done anything. It was going to hurt an awful lot for a long time to come, because he and Pa had been very close, but it wasn't anything that a man died of. He could take it.

By the time he had made a second trip to the well, Mrs. Tusten and Susan had appeared. He said good morning a little shyly, because he wasn't used to womenfolk. Once in a while he had seen girls when he went in to Minisink, but they hadn't been pretty girls like Susan. She had long, reddish-brown hair that fell to her shoulders in curls. Her face was oval and when she smiled he could see that her teeth were white and pretty, the way his mother's had been.

"Did you get a good night's sleep?" Mrs. Tusten asked. She was a small, tidy woman. Joel decided that he liked her.

"Yes, ma'am. And you?"

"The baby woke up twice," Mrs. Tusten said absently. "Oh, I forgot. You haven't met our whole family, Joel."

Just then the doctor came in carrying an infant and followed by three older children. "Good morning, Joel," he smiled. "I brought the rest of the family in for you to meet."

The tallest came around his father. "I'm James and I'm almost nine years old," he said. "How old are you?"

Joel grinned. "Almost sixteen."

James indicated the next in line with a gesture reminiscent of the doctor. "This is Thomas. He's only seven. And that's Sarah. She's three, and she was the baby until we got Abigail."

Joel forced himself to keep a straight face. "How do you do, Thomas? Sarah? And Abigail, of course."

James and Thomas burst into delighted laughter and Sarah buried her face in her mother's apron.

"Well, you've been accepted, Joel," Doctor Tusten smiled. "How about some breakfast?"

After breakfast, during which the three children shyly peeped at Joel when they thought he wasn't looking, he followed the doctor out to the barn, pausing once to look back at the white board house. It had a fine, substantial look to it, as if whoever had built it had meant to stay.

"Captain Brown will have his company out on patrol around the town this morning," the doctor said. "I want to meet with the other officers this morning over at the Reverend Hanley's house. Then I want to send a party out to Minisink, just to make sure the hostiles are still in the area. If you feel up to it, you might go along and return the horse to Jonas."

"Yes, sir."

They saddled quickly in the barn, the doctor helping Joel, and then they led the horses out into the chill gloom of the early dawn. Joel looked up at the sky and sniffed the air. "It's going to snow some more," he said.

"Wouldn't be surprised," Doctor Tusten replied. "You always seem to get the thing you need least."

At the Reverend Hanley's house, Captain Williamson and Sergeant Ford were waiting for them. The captain explained that Captain Brown was already assembling his company on the far edge of town and that Captain Harper had slipped on the ice and hurt his ankle and so could not come.

The Reverend Hanley looked distressed, as if somehow it was his fault that the errant captain had fallen. He was a thin, somewhat lugubrious man, a few years older than Doctor Tusten. He smiled warmly at Joel and introduced his son Adam, a tall, lanky boy of fourteen. "You and Adam can talk while the conference is going on," he said.

"Sorry, Parson," the doctor said. "Joel is going to tell us what happened. Perhaps Adam could stay and listen, too."

The reverend gentleman looked surprised. "Well, I think it would be all right. I mean to say, I suppose Adam should hear some of this as part of his education."

The doctor kept a straight face, but as he walked into the parlor after Adam and his father, he turned and smiled at Joel.

Captain Williamson was a barrel-chested man in homespun. His hair was plain, black, and hacked off short at the level of his ears. His assistant, Sergeant Ford, was thin as a rail and he wore his unpowdered, graying hair clubbed with an eelskin. He winked solemnly at Joel.

"Well, Joel," the doctor said after the introductions. "Suppose you tell us again what happened."

Joel told them.

Captain Williamson nodded when he was through. "I think the boy's right. It was a small party sent out to distract attention from some other place. The thing is, Brown's company ought to be big enough to handle them if he can catch them before they meet up with the main band."

The doctor shook his head. "Captain Brown isn't trying to catch them. He's merely patrolling the outskirts of the town to make sure they aren't lurking in the woods. I thought perhaps you could take over the defense of the stockade. Keep most of your company on call and let Sergeant Ford take a detail over to Minisink to see if they've heard anything further."

Captain Williamson nodded. "All right, Doc. How about the boy, here?"

"He can go along and return the horse to Jonas."

Adam Hanley looked enviously at Joel and then he turned to his father.

"No, Adam," the parson said. "This is man's work."

Joel smothered a grin. It was funny in a way, but it wasn't funny in another. A man never seemed to know how much it hurt a boy to be told he wasn't old enough for something he wanted to do.

Sergeant Ford stood up. "Well, I'll get started," he said. "I've got six men waiting. As long as we're careful, I don't think we'll have any trouble. Maybe we can come back by way of the Benton place and see if we can pick up trail."

"All right, Nathan," the doctor said. "Just don't walk into anything you can't handle."

The sergeant grinned. "They've got to get up early in the morning to catch me napping, Doc. I was fighting them twenty years ago, in the old French war."

Sergeant Ford was a gunsmith, clockmaker, and locksmith. He had also served with Rogers' Rangers in the French and Indian War. He told Joel all of that in the short walk down the street to his shop where the six men from his squad were waiting.

"You know anything about guns?" he asked Joel hopefully.

"Pa had a Golcher rifle," Joel said proudly. "I could take the lock apart and put it back together again."

"Well," Sergeant Ford said. "That's a fine thing to be

able to do. Maybe you're going to drive me out of business, though. Hey?"

"No, sir," Joel smiled. "I don't have the tools or the shop, for one thing."

"Hmm. Did you ever think about taking it up as a trade?"

"No, I guess not. Pa wanted me to be a lawyer or a doctor, but the only thing I ever had time to do was plant corn and hunt to keep us alive. I don't know what I'm going to do, now."

"Well," Sergeant Ford said. "We'll see what we'll see."

However much Sergeant Ford had bragged about his past war experiences with Rogers' Rangers, Joel had to admit that he knew his business. The six men fanned out into a diamond-shaped formation as soon as they left the outskirts of town. Ford stayed close to the center with two men fifty yards in front of him and two others fifty yards behind. The remaining two men marched at the sides.

At Joel's suggestion, they shared the horse, taking turn and turn about until they reached the outskirts of Minisink about three hours later. There were no tracks, but Sergeant Ford said he hadn't really expected to find any.

"In the first place, the snow could have covered them over here, because the land is pretty low. And in the second place, I don't think they came this way."

"Why not? They'd have to go north to get to Canada."

Ford grinned. "They knew they'd been spotted and even if they didn't they'd probably head for the river and try to follow it. They could head through the woods sticking to the high ground where there wouldn't be much snow and then follow the river on the ice where they could make good time. They say the river's froze solid beyond Fort Narrowsburg."

"I didn't think of that. That would put them on the west fork and they could follow that all the way to Unadilla, pretty near."

Ford nodded. "That's right, boy. And once they're at Unadilla, they've got friends and food to take care of them for the rest of the winter. Butler and Brant have been using it as a rendezvous right along."

Although there was a guard in the spy tower of the stockade, the houses around it showed signs of life and the big gate was ajar. Smoke was even coming from the big chimney of Jonas' store.

Ford shook his head in disgust. "Some people have short memories. They dang near got burned out last summer and here they don't even have an alarm out today."

Jonas was glad to see them. "Well, bub," he greeted Joel. "How do you feel this morning? Hey?"

"A lot better than I felt last night. I guess that ball didn't go in too deep. I can use the arm some."

"That's good," Jonas said heartily.

"What's the news of Indians?" Ford asked abruptly.

"Well, they sent out a patrol first thing in the morning and didn't come up with any tracks. I guess maybe the Indians took off down the Delaware and headed for home."

"How far out did the patrol go?"

"Three miles in every direction," Jonas said proudly. "I guess they was just a little party that got lost."

Ford grinned scornfully. "Not if they was Mohawks. Oneidas, maybe. Mohawks don't get lost. I figure they had orders to show themselves and stir up a little commotion to take the attention away from the main body. You mark my words, there's more to this than it looks like right now. And if you'll take my advice, you'll go on the alert until we find out where the rest of them are."

Jonas made a droll face at Joel as the sergeant walked out of the store. "Sure takes himself serious, don't he?" he murmured.

Joel looked at him.

Jonas suddenly flushed. "I'm sorry, bub. For a minute

there, I forgot it was you. And it's serious enough for you, ain't it?"

Joel nodded and then he followed Sergeant Ford outside.

Ford put Joel in the lead as they left the village. "You know the way," he said. "Just be careful and keep that pistol ready in case you have to use it."

It was cold enough so that the walking was easy. Even the snow that had fallen during the night was frozen hard and they moved out quickly, past the house where he had fallen the night before, and into the long expanse of cleared land beyond. Joel could make out the tracks of the two Indians who had pursued him without too much trouble. The snow had drifted over them, but their outlines showed bluish-gray against the new snow.

Once they began the climb, the tracks were even clearer because the wind had swept the new snow away as fast as it had fallen, but when they reached the top of the ridge and started down the other side the tracks faded into nothingness and he realized that there would be no chance of picking up the trail until they reached the clearing.

He held up his hand for a halt at the rock where he had stopped to rest just before he heard the shots. Sergeant Ford came up to him. "See anything?" he asked.

"I stopped to rest here and when I heard the shooting I threw my bundle off to the side so I could pick it up later."

Ford nodded. "Remember where you threw it?"

Joel looked towards the low bushes he remembered. It was over in there some place, he was pretty certain. "I think it's in here," he said.

He went over to the bushes and stamped around. A scrap of deerskin stuck up out of the snow. It was frozen stiff. He knelt down and tugged at it and it came free. There was

39

nothing else. The flour sack had apparently been slit and emptied by the Indians, perhaps by the third man, who had turned back. He saw it now, fluttering from the branches of a nearby tree. The bladder containing the molasses was gone. So were the powder and the lead.

"Was that it?" Ford asked.

"That was it," he said. It wasn't the loss of the goods he minded so much. It was the loss of the hot days hoeing corn and the cold, rainy day last spring when he had tracked a buck for ten miles before he could get a good shot at him. It was time and sweat and disappointment and the illusion of triumph that became failure. It hurt.

"Too bad," Ford said sympathetically, but he stamped his feet with ill-disguised impatience. In a way he was right, Joel thought. There was nothing to be gained by crying over an irretrievable loss.

"Well, we might as well start out," Joel said.

They went the last half-mile up the ridge and he thought to himself: This is the last time I'll come up this ridge and expect to see the house the way it was. I know it's gone, and I even saw it burning, but I can still remember it more the way it was before than the way I saw it yesterday.

They came to the crest of the ridge and then Ford touched his arm. "We'll wait up here, just in case." He told off four men to go down the slope and across the creek and examine the clearing.

"It wouldn't be the first time the devils have come back to pick up a few easy scalps from a burial party," he explained.

Joel nodded. "I guess that's right. I could go down there with them, though."

"No," Ford said decisively. "You don't want to see what's down there."

The four men walked up the cornfield with long, easy strides. One of them had slung his rifle by the straps and held his hand axe in his right hand. Apparently he intended

40

to hack a grave out of the frozen ground. Joel bit his lower lip and stared at the glittering blade of the axe.

The four men circled the clearing looking for tracks and then they went over to where the smoke-blacked chimney stood naked above the ashes of the walls. The man with the hand axe went around to the rear of the chimney and began to hack at the ground with quick, light strokes. He doesn't want to hit a rock and turn the edge of his blade, Joel thought. A little pile of sods grew as they watched and then another man came over and took a turn. After that, the four went over to a corner of the cabin and bent down.

"Don't look," Ford said with a harsh voice. "It's over and done with.There's nothing there for you now."

Joel nodded and looked down at the snow between his feet. He could feel the tears wet on his face and hear the wind singing faintly in the hemlock stand up on the ridge. And then Ford touched him on the shoulder.

"All right," the sergeant said. "They want us to come down there, now."

The burial party had made a neat grave, packing the sods in even rows and banking them down with stones from the foundation. The man with the axe came over to Joel. "You can come and put a marker on it when it's warmer," he said. "Maybe cut his name and all on it."

"Yes," Joel said. The remains of Pa's surveying instruments lay near the chimney. The tripods were broken, and the transit had been smashed.

"There wasn't a lot left," the man continued. "It must have been a hot fire."

Joel stared at him and then the man nodded and walked away as if he had just remembered something he had to do in a hurry.

"All right," Ford said briskly. "Did anybody find tracks?"

"Plenty of them where the wind blew the snow away. Most of them head down to the creek, though."

41

Just to make sure, they circled the clearing again. The hostiles had started out towards the north when Joel had observed them the day before, but they had apparently altered course and headed straight for the creek.

"Maybe they were all going to follow me," Joel suggested.

Ford shook his head. "I don't think so. They probably told the ones that chased you to meet them further down. They wanted to follow the creek until it hit the river, because the ice would be solid pretty near all the way and the snow would cover their tracks quickly. What does that mean to you?"

Joel knew that the sergeant was deliberately trying to get his mind off the burial of his father and the horror that had preceded it, but he didn't mind. It made no sense brooding over it. Now: the Indians had gone down the creek to cover their tracks. Why? He thought about it for a moment.

"Well, they knew that I had seen them and that somebody would find me even if they caught me. So there was no point in trying to keep anybody from knowing they were here. The thing it means is probably that they were too small a party to stand and fight anything bigger than a very small party like ours. All they had to do was show themselves to tie us down. They've done that, so they're running for Canada, the quickest way they can."

"Good boy," Ford approved. "That's the way to read a sign. We'll go down to the creek and see if they left any kind of trail coming out. I doubt it, but it never hurts to make sure."

But although they followed the creek along the top of the ridge for two miles they failed to see any tracks. At the end of half an hour, Ford went down to the surface of the ice and painstakingly swept away the snow until he found what he wanted. He pointed out the trail to Joel.

"See? The slush was soft and took prints, because it was still early enough in the afternoon. They came up the

42

creek and they went back the same way." He studied the moccasin prints, vague and blurred around the edges. "Hard to tell what they were. Probably Mohawks, if the officer was one of Butler's men."

But Joel was looking at the odd track that was somewhat to the side of the others. The prints were sharply outlined with crisp edges and there was a separate heelprint for each of them. They were made by a cobbled boot, especially soled for hard usage. An Army boot. The boot of the officer in the green coat.

The boot of the man who wore a white cockade in his black skullcap.

Ford nodded to Joel. "That's him, all right," he said, reading Joel's mind.

"That's the man I'm going to kill," Joel said.

FIVE

IT was already growing dark by the time Sergeant Ford's patrol reached the outskirts of Goshen, because the sergeant had taken a wide swing to the south of town to make sure that the patrol sent out by Captain Brown had "done its job," as he put it.

"I'll take the other men in to town and report to the captain directly," Ford said. "Why don't you cut along back to the doctor's place? If he's there, you can tell him for me I reported to the captain and you can tell him what we found. Or what we didn't find."

Joel nodded. He was more tired than he cared to admit. "All right, Sergeant. I'll tell him when I see him."

"That's fine. It'll save me a trip out there later. Besides, I'll have a lot of work to catch up on tonight. I promised Pete Schneider I'd get his lock fixed by tomorrow."

"A lock's not going to do much good against Indians."

"That's a fact," Ford agreed. "But Pete thinks it is. If you don't have anything to do tomorrow, why don't you come around to the shop?"

"All right. I'd like to."

Sergeant Ford waved a bony hand and trudged off through the snow, followed by his detail.

Joel saw the lights of the Tusten house shining through the trees just as if there weren't an Indian within fifty miles of the town. He wondered why they didn't take the raid seriously and then he remembered how he had confidently told Pa only yesterday morning that the Indians were all back in

Canada, holed up against the winter. Somehow, you never quite believed a thing until it happened to you.

He turned into the yard and went around the back to the kitchen door and knocked.

"Who's there, please?" He recognized Susan's voice.

"Joel Benton."

There was a pause and then she spoke again. "What's my name?"

"Susan. Susan North."

The bolt on the door slid back with an oily click and then the door opened to show Susan standing there, holding an antiquated blunderbuss in her left hand. He changed his mind about the unpreparedness of the Tusten household.

"Come in," she said shyly.

"Don't shoot me with that thing," he grinned.

She laughed in pretty confusion. "Uncle Ben wants us to keep a gun handy when we go to the door nowadays. Even when people know your name, sometimes it isn't safe. They might have heard it from someone and tell it to you just to get inside the house."

"That's so," he said solemnly. "I never thought of that."

"Aunt Catherine is upstairs taking a nap with Sarah. The baby just about wears her out. The boys are playing doctor."

He nodded, not knowing quite how to begin. Perhaps she didn't know whether he was supposed to stay here tonight or not. The doctor didn't look like the kind of man who would turn anybody away on a cold night, but nothing had been said about it in the morning.

"Are you hungry?" Susan asked.

"I could eat if you forced me to," he smiled. "I haven't had anything since breakfast."

"I have some stew in the pot," Susan said. She went to fetch a plate from the cupboard. It was a fine-looking piece, made out of oiled pine, and it reminded him a little of his mother's cupboard that had been burned when the Tories came, two years ago.

"Sergeant Ford told me he was going in to town with the others. He wanted to tell the doctor what we found."

Susan nodded. "You're staying with us, you know."

"No, I didn't."

"Well, where in the world else would you go? Uncle Ben never turns anyone away."

"I figured as much," Joel said with relief. "Only I wasn't sure."

She brought a steaming plate over to the table. "Uncle Ben rode in to the village about an hour ago. I think he went to see Captain Brown. He ought to be back any time now." She cut a slice of bread from a brown loaf and put it near his plate. "Did you find anything of the Indians?"

He shook his head and swallowed a mouthful. "Nothing but tracks. They took off down the creek and headed for the river. They might have hit Lackawaxen, across the Delaware, but I don't think so. I think they're headed out for Canada as fast as they can go."

"Did they—did they have any prisoners?"

He looked at her directly. "If you mean Pa, no," he said gently. "Some of the men found him and buried him. He didn't make it. I knew he couldn't have."

She looked down and he noticed that her eyes were bright with tears. "I'm sorry," she said.

"That's mighty kind of you, Susan." He said her name with a kind of relish. It was a pretty name, when you came to think about it.

"What will you do?"

He grinned. "Well, I might go up to my Uncle Charley's place and see if I could help out there. He's got a farm up in the Cherry Valley. The only thing is, they probably don't have too much to eat and it's a long trip in the middle of winter. I guess the other thing I could do is try to get in the army. They might not notice my age."

47

"I'm sure they wouldn't," Susan said loyally.

"On the other hand, I could try to find some work around here in return for my keep. That would hold me over until spring, and then I could make up my mind."

"Oh, yes," Susan said. "I'm sure Uncle Ben would be able to find something for you. He knows everybody in the county and there isn't anyone who wouldn't be glad to do him a favor."

Joel finished his plate of stew and put down his spoon. He was beginning to feel better, now. His buckskins were drying out in the heat radiating from the fireplace and his arm didn't seem to hurt too much, either. He felt a sharp jab in his ribs as he leaned forward and then he remembered the pistol in his belt. He pulled it out and laid it on top of the mantelpiece. It ought to be safe from the children there.

"One of Uncle Ben's patients gave him those pistols. There are two of them, made in England."

"They look mighty handsome," Joel said. "They use the same lock as most of the muskets, though."

Someone knocked on the door and Susan looked at him. "It must be Uncle Ben," she said. "But . . ."

"Best make sure," he told her. He picked up the pistol and pulled the hammer back with his left hand. Then he motioned her towards the door.

"Who is it?"

They waited for a breathless moment.

"Uncle Ben, Susan. Is Joel Benton home yet?"

"Yes, sir," he called. "Right here."

Susan slid back the lock and then he lowered the pistol as he recognized the doctor.

Doctor Tusten patted Susan on the head and divested himself of his greatcoat. "Turning colder," he said heartily. "I'm glad no babies are due for the next week."

Joel smiled.

"It's no laughing matter," the doctor said. "They always seem to time their arrival into this world at the least convenient—or comfortable—time for the doctor."

48

"I didn't think of it that way," Joel admitted. "Sergeant Ford told me to report to you. He took the patrol in and he was going to report to Captain Brown himself."

The doctor nodded. "I saw Sergeant Ford myself, just after he got in. I wanted to talk to him about something else, so I got the report from him directly. Did you eat?"

Joel flushed. "Yes, sir. I'm sorry. I should have waited."

"Never apologize for an empty belly, Joel. It's a natural state of man. The only thing to do about it is fill it. And I propose to do just that."

"Aunt Catherine's taking a nap, Uncle Ben. She said to call her when you came home."

"Quite right, Susan. Would you call her now?"

When Susan had gone off to the narrow stairway in the hall, the doctor turned to Joel. "I wanted to see Sergeant Ford about something other than the patrol," he said cheerfully. "He told me that you were a great help today."

"That was mighty kind of him," Joel said, flushing with pleasure.

"Stuff! Nathan Ford doesn't give compliments unless they're earned. He said that you guessed what the raiders had done before anyone else."

"It seemed pretty clear to me, sir."

The doctor smiled. "A great many things that seem clear to an intelligent man are quite muddy to one less intelligent, Joel."

"Well, sir. It's like the lock on a rifle, for example. If you pull back the hammer, the spring squeezes together. When you pull the trigger, the spring lets go and the hammer flies down. Any time you do something, it's bound to have a result somewhere. The only hard part is to figure out the result somehow."

"I'm glad you brought that up, Joel. Ford needs help with his repair work. What with the militia being liable to service in winter as well as summer, now that the Indians have extended their raiding season, more firearms are in need of repair and there are fewer qualified men to repair them.

Ford told me that he thought you knew something about guns. How would you like to work for him?"

Joel smiled. "Well, sir. I would like to, except for one thing. My father always wanted me to go to school to learn to be a lawyer or a doctor. I'd like to do what he wanted me to."

The doctor frowned. "What do you want to do?"

"I want to be a doctor, sir."

"It takes more than wanting, Joel. You have to want to be a good doctor. There are too many doctors in the profession who just want to make money and let their patients go hang."

Joel thought about it. "I guess I'd want to be good no matter what profession it was. I took care of Pa during the last year and I liked doing it. Not just because it was Pa, but because he was someone who was sick and needed help and I was able to help him. Do you know what I mean?"

"I know," the doctor said with satisfaction. "That's the right way to begin."

"Well, sir. Now that I've got a start, how do I keep on going?"

Doctor Tusten looked amused. "One way would be to take the job with Ford. That would give you a place to live and food to eat. Maybe you could come out here and study with me for a while."

He felt a warm glow spreading in him. "That would be fine, sir. I never dreamed . . ."

"Stuff," the doctor said. "It'll be hard work and I warn you now! I'm a hard taskmaster!"

"Yes, sir!" Joel said happily.

After supper, the doctor sat back from the table with James on one knee and Thomas on the other. Mrs. Tusten held the baby, Abigail, while Sarah stood across the room shyly inspecting Joel.

He pretended not to notice her and picked up a piece of wood, selecting it carefully for grain. Out of the corner of his eye he could see that she was watching every move he made. He took out his sheath knife and began to whittle so that the chips fell on the hearth.

After a while, the stick of wood began to resemble a doll. At least, he thought, it's got two arms and one head and a long skirt. He held it up as if to examine it and he noticed that Sarah had stepped into the room to see it more closely.

"That's a fine doll you're making, Joel," Mrs. Tusten said with concealed amusement. "Are you making it for some one special?"

"Well, ma'am, I just hadn't made up my mind. Of course Susan might like to have it, only I guess she's too big to play with dolls."

"That's so," Mrs. Tusten said gravely. "How about the baby?"

"Well, I don't know about the baby. She might be a little young to play with dolls just yet. I guess I'll just have to say whoever wants it can have it."

"Me!" Thomas shouted.

James gave him a scornful look. "Boys don't play with dolls. They play with soldiers."

"I guess they do at that," Joel said. "I'll tell you what. I can maybe make a couple of soldiers. Would you like that?"

Thomas smiled shyly, but James frowned. "I want a horse."

Joel nodded. "That's a tall order, but I guess I can handle it." He cleared his throat. "The point is, what can I do with this doll?"

"Give it to me?" Sarah asked wistfully.

"Why, I never thought of that. You're just the one that ought to have it!"

Sarah smiled shyly.

"You want to come and get it?"

"No!" She laughed teasingly.

"I'll tell you what I'll do then. I'll put it down in the middle of the floor and you can take it from there. All right?"

Sarah nodded and he put the doll down. As soon as he had returned to the hearth she ran over and seized it.

"What do you say when someone gives you something?" the doctor prompted.

"I don't know," Sarah teased.

"You'd better try to think of it."

Suddenly she skipped across the room to Joel and planted a kiss on his cheek. "Thank you, Joel!" she shouted. And then she ran back to her corner clutching her new acquisition.

The grownups began to laugh and then James and Thomas joined in. It was a warm family, Joel thought. A good home. Like the one I had. And then he remembered. It could be taken away any time by a bullet or a blazing torch or a tomahawk.

The knocking at the door cut off the laughter like a knife. The boys sprang away from their father and Joel went over to the mantelpiece for the pistol.

"Who's there?" the doctor called out.

"Dispatch from Colonel Hathorn for Colonel Tusten."

"Identify yourself."

"Pete Schneider, Doc. Captain Brown sent me over."

The doctor nodded and Joel put the pistol back on the mantelpiece. The doctor crossed to the door and opened it.

Pete Schneider was a small, thin, worried man. If he was the same one who wanted his lock by tomorrow, Joel thought, that would account for it. A man like that would want to keep everything under lock and key. He handed the doctor a sealed paper. The doctor opened the paper and read it. Then he looked up.

"My compliments to Captain Brown," he said. "His company can go off alert and Captain Williamson's can take over. No other change in orders."

"All right, Doc," Schneider said.

"Tell Captain Brown to spread the word. Butler and Brant and their Tories and Indians hit Cherry Valley the day before yesterday. The way it looks, they wiped out the whole settlement."

"I'll tell him, Doc." Pete Schneider looked around for a moment, perhaps hoping to be asked to stay and have a glass of beer. Then he turned to the door. "Goodnight," he said.

The door closed behind Pete and Joel stepped away from the mantel, as carefully as if he were walking on broken glass. "I'd better start out in the morning," he said.

The doctor looked at him and shook his head. "It wouldn't do any good, boy. If your uncle and his family weren't killed, they'd be half-way up to Niagara by the time you got there."

"But I can't just do nothing!"

"Sometimes that's all there is to do. You can do this much. Join the militia right now and learn the drill. Keep yourself in condition. Learn whatever Ford can teach you and whatever I can teach you. Be ready so that when the time comes you'll be ready for it."

He nodded. "Yes, sir. Only it seems hard, somehow. I think I'd like to go outside and take a walk around."

Mrs. Tusten nodded her approval. "That's a good idea. When you come back, we'll have a cup of tea and then to bed."

Out in the cold, crisp night the stars wheeled in circles of icy fire. The air was clean and fresh and he could pick up the individual odors without any trouble. The smell of the horses in the barn. The fresher smell of Schneider's nag. The faint odor of wood smoke from the chimney. And the pepper smell of extreme cold.

So that had been the meaning of the small party down here. It had been a diversion, after all, designed to keep the small force of regulars moving from one place to another, where they would wear themselves out and be out of the way when the time came to strike. Designed to inspire terror. What was it the Bible said? "Thou shalt not be afraid for the terror by night; nor for the arrow that flieth by day; nor for the pestilence that walketh in darkness; nor for the destruction that wasteth at noon-day."

Well, he was afraid for the terror and so were a lot of other people. Only now he only had to be afraid for himself, because there was nobody left at all, now. No. That wasn't true, either. He had to be afraid for the doctor's family and Susan, because he had them now instead of a family of his own. It wasn't quite the same, but it was almost as good.

He turned around and went back to the door.

SIX

AS the doctor saddled his horse the next morning, he did some serious thinking. It was odd the way a man could sit in a quiet room and try to think and never get anywhere, he thought with a trace of amusement. It seemed that the best time to think was when you were doing something with your hands. Right now, he had solved the problem of Joel in two minutes.

He turned to the boy and smiled. "All set?"

"Yes, sir."

"I've had an idea. Remember Adam Hanley? The parson's son? Well, he's a fair scholar, but he knows next to nothing about the woods. Now I was thinking that he could help you learn mathematics, and you could take him out hunting with you and teach him some woodcraft. Besides, it would be good exercise for both of you."

"That sounds fine," Joel said. "If Adam wants to."

"I'm sure he will," Doctor Tusten replied. "Adam's main problem has been that he has no brothers or sisters, and being the parson's son makes it difficult for him to make friends."

"Well, I'd like to try, sir."

"Good. The next thing is Latin. You can't hope to be a doctor unless you know Latin, because all your medicines have Latin names. After you know your Latin, then we can go further and you may accompany me on calls and help me make up prescriptions. Gradually, you can learn all that I can teach you and by that time you should have enough money to spend a year or two with another doctor and become licensed."

"Yes, sir," Joel said. His eyes were shining with hope. "How do I study Latin, sir?"

"You can come out to the house two nights a week with Adam and learn from me. The parson will help you some, too, but I don't believe he knows as much Latin as I do."

Joel laughed happily. "I can't remember when I've felt so good about the way things are going."

Doctor Tusten felt a sharp pang. There were so many things that could go wrong before Joel attained his goal. Would he find the obstacles insurmountable? Would he give up without trying hard enough? Somehow he didn't think so. But it wasn't fair not to warn the boy.

"It won't all be easy, Joel. You're going to have to do a lot of memorizing. You'll have to know the name of every bone and organ in the body. Maybe you won't be able to do it. What will you do then?"

Joel smiled at him with complete assurance. "If that happens, sir, I'll know that I wasn't meant to be a doctor and I'll try to be as good as I can in some other field."

There wasn't any point in saying anything in answer to such an affirmative declaration of faith. The doctor put out his hand. "Shake on it," he said gruffly.

Adam was a shy, thin boy and, as the doctor had predicted, he was only too glad to have the opportunity to go out in the woods with someone his own age. Joel wondered silently whether Adam would ever be strong enough to hunt through an entire day without stopping. But he said nothing of this.

"I can use my father's fowling piece," Adam said happily. "He said he'd let me, if I could find someone to take me."

Joel smiled. "Well, it's a lot better than the gun I haven't got. Our rifle was stolen by the Tory." His throat tightened and he couldn't speak for a moment. Then he went bravely on. "The one who killed my father."

56

"Doctor Tusten said you were going to work for Mr. Ford. Maybe he'll let you take a musket. He must have a lot of them."

"Maybe," Joel replied dubiously, watching the doctor gesturing as he talked to Adam's father.

"The doctor said you knew a lot about guns. That ought to make it easy for you to learn mathematics."

"Why is that?"

Adam warmed to a subject near to his heart. "Well, all mathematics is really clear, logical thinking. If you can see why the hammer falls on a gun lock when you pull the trigger, then you know logic."

Joel remembered his conversation with the doctor last night. He had used the very same thing to explain his quick appraisal of the probable destination of the raiding party.

"You can come over here and study Latin with me whenever Mr. Ford will let you," Adam was saying. "I've only been working on it for a year, so I won't be too far ahead of you."

"That would be fine," Joel said slowly. "I was just thinking. I haven't had a friend since my folks left Edmeston three years ago. My pa was a good patriot; but most of the folks there were Tory, and they burned us out."

"That's awful," Adam said. "I'm glad we don't have any Tories around here."

"So am I," the parson said. He and the doctor had finished their conversation and had come closer to the boys.

Doctor Tusten's eyes were quizzical. "With all due respect, Parson, I wouldn't be too sure of that. Many a man right here in town would show his true colors tomorrow, if a King's Army were to march in."

"Heaven forbid!"

The doctor smiled at Joel. "Amen to that," he said.

Adam looked at Joel. "Maybe you could come over tonight. We could talk about mathematics some. And I could show you some Latin."

"I'd like that a lot, Adam. I want to get started just

as soon as I can. I'll come if it's all right with Mr. Ford."

It was obvious that everything was going to be all right with Nathan Ford. As soon as they opened the door to the tiny shop he greeted them with a big grin. "Well, come in! Come in out of the cold!"

"How are you this morning, Nate?"

"Just fine, Doc. Fit as a fiddle."

"I brought Joel over. Unless you've changed your mind, he can stay here."

"No, Doc. I haven't changed my mind a whit. How about you, Joel? Do you think you want to be a gunsmith?"

"I want to be a doctor, Mr. Ford. But I'll try to be a good apprentice while I'm here."

"That's the talk," Nathan Ford said heartily. "The terms are, you work every day except Sunday from when you get up in the morning until after supper. You can hunt for us one day a week. You get off muster day, too."

"That sounds fine," Joel said.

"Don't you want to know the other side of the bargain?" Mr. Ford chuckled.

"I guess I would," Joel said sheepishly.

"Well, you can sleep in the back of the shop here. There's a bunk in the corner with a shelf over it. The missus and me, we used to sleep here before we built the other two rooms on. We'll feed you good and pay you a shilling a month besides."

Joel smiled and stuck out his hand. "It's a bargain."

"Well, that's fine, then. The only other thing is, you can use my second-best musket and you can have powder and ball for hunting and for muster. There won't be no charge for that."

Doctor Tusten smiled. "Don't give everything away, Nate."

"Don't you worry about it, Doc. How about a glass of beer before you go?"

"No, thanks. I have some calls to make and then I have

58

to get back home and put up prescriptions. It wouldn't do to see double." Doctor Tusten turned to Joel. "You'll come out with Adam tomorrow night, then?"

"Yes, sir. I'll be looking forward to it."

The doctor smiled at him. "So will Susan," he said.

Joel felt the blood rush to his face. He hadn't said a word about Susan, but the doctor seemed to know all about how he had been thinking that it would be nice if she happened to be around when he came out for lessons.

When the doctor had gone, Nathan Ford introduced Joel to Mrs. Ford, a kindly, plump, gray-haired lady in her early fifties. "Bless me, it'll be nice to have somebody else to talk to," she said. "Nate just has two things on his mind, his shop and the militia company. The rest of the world could go hang for all of him, I do believe."

Mr. Ford grinned. "That's the way of a woman, Joel. Always complaining. When they don't, they ain't happy."

The Ford house had been built a little at a time. The original house had been a one-room log structure with a fireplace on one side. Then a two-room ell had been built on alongside the fireplace wall. The original room had been sheathed with boards on the outside to match the newer ell, and it now housed the shop. One of the newer rooms served as a general room for living, and the other room was the Fords' bedroom.

The shop interested Joel most. Mr. Ford kept his tools on neat shelves and on a counter that ran down the length of the room. It was a clean place, smelling of oil and metal and solder. There was a small anvil and a bellows near the fireplace where Mr. Ford told him that he forged small parts for broken locks.

Under the bunk in the rear of the shop, Mr. Ford kept a large supply of lead and powder. "They called most of it in," he confided to Joel. "But I saved some back. You never know when you might need a little extra."

Mr. Ford's rifle, a real Kentucky-made piece, hung on

pegs over the bunk. Under it, two British Army muskets occupied secondary positions of honor. "Captured in the raid last summer," Mr. Ford said briefly.

"Who captured them?"

Mr. Ford chuckled. "I did. I was with Rogers in fifty-nine on the St. Francis raid. I'm not so old yet I've forgotten how to get behind an Indian in the woods." He pointed to the lower musket. "You can use this one. It's in better shape than the other. I don't know where the Indian who owned it got it. The British generally don't give them muskets. There's some say that the Indians sometimes fight with the British when there's nobody else handy. Maybe that's where it came from."

A week later, in his role as sergeant, Nathan Ford swore Joel into the militia as a private. He was to be in Ford's company and Ford promised him that he would use him as a scout.

"I don't know but what you couldn't have kept up with the Rangers back in fifty-eight," Ford said. It was the highest praise he ever gave anyone. He followed it with a detailed instruction of musket-loading, military fashion, and with a description of the various movements a body of troops might be expected to make on command. Then he grinned at Joel and told him that it all held good only on muster day.

"The rest of the time, if we go out, you'll do what comes naturally. I don't see that it hurt the Indians any, not knowing Right Wheel from Present Arms. They're pretty good fighters without knowing all this stuff."

"I guess Doctor Tusten wants it that way, though," Joel said.

Mr. Ford shook his head. "He's a born soldier, the Doc is. He only got voted in as Lieutenant Colonel last year, you know. Before that, he didn't know anything about drill. He just does it because Colonel Hathorn wants it, but he has a lot of common sense. That goes a long ways in Indian fighting. Rogers would've liked the Doc just fine."

"How did he get to be a doctor?"

"Oh, that. Well, the old Colonel, the Doc's father, he was a farmer and a pretty rich one at that. He wanted Doc to be a farmer, too, but when Doc was a boy he was sickly, so the Colonel sent him to school back east on Long Island. He was there for two-three years studying mathematics and Latin and Greek and that stuff, and then he came back here and studied doctoring under old Doctor Wickham. He's dead, now. Then Doc went off to New Jersey to study under another doctor there. That's where he met his wife. After that, he went to New York City to learn surgery and then he came back here and got married and started practicing."

"Then he was rich to start with?" Joel asked with a sense of disappointment.

Ford nodded. "He had money, all right. The thing is, though, he could have just been an ordinary kind of doctor if that's all he'd wanted. But he worked at being the best kind of doctor he knew how. He didn't have to go study surgery. And he could have let the whole danged Valley keep right on having smallpox. But he didn't. He went and gave eight hundred people cowpox so they couldn't catch the other. Now just think of that!"

"It seems to me that everybody'd want to have cowpox if it would keep them from getting smallpox."

"Not around here," Ford replied. "They were all against it. You know the kind: if my daddy had smallpox, then I ought to have it, too. They never want to change. But the Doc, he bullied them and jollied them until they came in to be fixed up just so they could get rid of him."

"How did they feel about it afterwards?"

Ford laughed. "Well, that turned the corner for the Doc. Once folks saw that nobody was getting the smallpox any more, they realized he'd staked his whole reputation just to keep them well. There wasn't a thing they wouldn't do for him then. There's nobody in the county better liked than Doc."

Gradually, the picture of the doctor emerged. A man of high principle, yet tolerant of the shortcomings of others. A dedicated man, not showing off his superior mind or his extensive knowledge to others, but helping them, serving them as best he could. And me, too, Joel thought. He didn't have to volunteer to teach me any more than he had to see Mr. Ford about a job for me. He could have kept me on at his place for a week or two until my arm healed and then let me go fend for myself.

It was a constant inspiration to Joel as he studied with Adam or with Adam and the doctor in the long winter nights. It didn't matter any more that the doctor had been a rich man. What did matter was that he had worked as hard as the poorest student in order to make himself the best doctor he could.

But there were two sides to everything. One part of Joel resented being shut up in the shop, working with things instead of people. He had been shut up in a cabin on the mountainside for too long not to appreciate the society of other humans. And again, he remembered with nostalgia the days of hunting, when he had been free to decide when to go and when to return. The old freedom was gone, and he regretted its passing.

But the main thing that bothered him was the thought that the Indians who had killed his father were still unpunished. There were men like the legendary Tom Quick who did something about it. Tom Quick's father had been killed by Indians he had once befriended, and Quick had sworn to kill a hundred Indians in vengeance.

Parson Hanley sniffed when Joel told him. " 'He that killeth with the sword must be killed with the sword,' " he said. "The man's nothing but a murderer. He's killed Indian women and children, and peaceful men as well as warriors. Faugh!"

"But we're apt to kill Indians in the militia service," Joel protested.

"That's in defense of our homes and our own families. It's a different thing than going out and killing without any reason but revenge."

Even Adam, who had become a good friend by this time, was against it. "I can see how you feel, Joel," he said as they returned home from a hunt. "You'd like to punish the men who were responsible for your father's death. Maybe I'd feel the same way, if it were me. But then you'd be as bad as they were."

Joel put down the haunch of the deer they had killed. "Let's take a breather," he said. "Why shouldn't they be punished?"

Adam smiled. "Because they were only fighting for what we took away from them. That's why people say the Indians are unreliable. One day they fight for the British, and the next day they might be fighting on our side. They're really fighting for their land; the land we took away from them."

"Well, we could make better use of it," Joel said stubbornly.

"That doesn't make it right. It's over now, and there's no way of giving it back to them without hurting a lot of us more. Besides, there's room enough for everybody. But that doesn't change the first point at all: we started the wrong."

"Well," Joel said as he scuffed at the snow with his moccasin. "There's one thing for sure. I'm not going to call it quits until I get the Tory who was with them. He's on the wrong side. Will you admit that?"

"Yes," Adam said reluctantly. "I'll admit that."

SEVEN

ADAM was unusually quiet, Joel decided. They had been studying together for a month now, and the longer they were together, the less Adam had to say about anything except Latin and mathematics.

Tonight they were working together at the deal table in the parson's kitchen. Parson Hanley and Mrs. Hanley were comfortably seated to either side of the wide fireplace.

"Ego," Joel said. "Ego, mihi, me, me."

"You missed the genitive," Adam said patiently. "Mei. Remember?"

"Oh. Yes, I've got it. Ego, mei, mihi, me, me."

Adam nodded. "Now the plural?"

Joel frowned. "Is there anything the matter, Adam? Are you angry about something?"

Adam smiled apologetically. "No, Joel. I suppose it's just that I've been feeling sorry for myself."

"You?" Joel was surprised. "If I knew Latin and mathematics the way you do, I'd think I was pretty special."

"They're not everything," Adam said. "I can't remember a squirrel's track from a bluejay's. I shot at a deer and I almost hit you."

Joel chuckled. "Well, you missed me, didn't you? That ought to be some consolation. Besides, you can't learn it all over night. It takes time."

"Well, perhaps it does. But I wish it didn't take so much."

Joel thought about it for a moment. Adam was still awkward in the woods, but he was learning steadily. He shouldn't be discouraged. Something must have happened. Or was it that something was going to happen? He racked his brain. The only thing that was going to happen was muster day. That came up tomorrow.

"Is it that you wish you were in the militia?" he asked Adam.

Adam nodded. "You don't know what it's like not to be counted in."

"I know it doesn't do any good saying so, but I had to wait, too. You see, we all can't be chosen at one time. We can't do much about it except use the time we have to wait in getting ready."

Adam frowned. It was obvious that he didn't feel much like waiting.

"What we could do is go over some of the drill after I learn it. With that and your hunting, you ought to be in a lot better shape than most of them by next year."

"Well," Adam said reluctantly, "I just wish everything didn't take so long."

It was extremely cold the next morning. Joel and Mr. Ford worked in the shop until almost ten, standing near the fire to keep warm. When Mrs. Ford came to the door leading into the ell to say that it was seventeen minutes to ten and hadn't they better get started, Mr. Ford winked at Joel.

"It's time to go out and get cold, boy," he said.

"Whose time do they go by?"

"Mine, generally. I'm ten minutes faster than the colonel, and he's five minutes faster than Captain Brown. If they go by mine, there's no danger of being late. You see, anybody who don't show up on time gets fined a shilling."

Joel was impressed. A shilling was a month's wages, if you didn't count the food and the bed. "I guess I won't have trouble about being late if I'm with you," he said.

"I guess you won't." The sergeant pulled on his outer

coat, made of the skin of a black bear. It wasn't the handsomest coat Joel had ever seen, but he guessed it ought to keep anybody warm.

He pulled on his own coat, which he had made last winter of deerskin with the hair left on, and followed the sergeant out into the cold morning.

The men were assembling in the square near the church when Sergeant Ford and Joel appeared. Most of Captain Brown's company was already together in a ragged sort of group, but the others were still milling around, greeting neighbors and joking about the coming drill.

"I got to go to the captain now," Sergeant Ford said. "You just fall in at the end of the line and do whatever the man next to you does."

Joel grinned and went over to the line. At first he was shy, because he saw that the man next to him was in his thirties and some of the other men were older than Sergeant Ford. But then he saw that there were boys in some of the other squads who weren't much older than he was. Apparently, that was one good thing about the militia; you could always find someone like yourself.

Two horsemen entered the square from the south. One was Doctor Tusten, wearing his blue cloak and heavy cowhide boots against the freezing weather. The other man was smartly dressed in the uniform of the Regular Army. His horseman's black cloak was thrown back to expose the blue uniform underneath, which was faced with buff lapels. He wore tanned deerskin breeches with polished black boots and a black tricorne hat. A smallsword hung at his side. If it weren't for the arrogant face beneath the hat, Joel thought, he might be a handsome man.

"Ho!" the next man in line said, nudging Joel in the ribs. "Look at the macaroni!"

"Who is he?"

"Danged if I know. Never saw him before."

The doctor and the strange officer reined in on the far

side of the square and the sergeants called their companies to attention.

Sergeant Ford grounded his rifle and bawled out: "Captain Brown's Company! Attention!"

The man next to Joel stood up straight and watched Sergeant Ford. He held his musket in front of him with both hands, the butt grounded. Joel imitated him and looked at Sergeant Ford.

The sergeant turned about smartly and shouldered his rifle. Then he saluted Captain Brown. "All present or accounted for, sir."

Captain Brown looked quizzical. "How do you know, Nate? You didn't call roll."

"I seen them when I come over," Sergeant Ford replied. "Everybody's here except Tom Harris, he cut his foot on an axe. And Paul Korven. He's got the chills and fever."

"All right, Nate. I'll inspect them." The captain walked over to Joel's end of the line, followed by Sergeant Ford. The latter had a notebook and a sharpened bullet to note irregularities. You got fined if everything wasn't in apple-pie order, Joel remembered. He was glad he had cleaned his musket last night.

"Hold it up so's he can see it," the man next to him advised.

Joel held the musket up and the captain took it away from him and looked at it. "Looks all right, Nate," he said. "Run the ramrod down it, son."

Joel slid the ramrod out of the clamps and thrust it down the barrel. "All right," the captain said. "Powder and ball all right?" He shook the powder horn and looked in Joel's pouch to make sure that he had the fifty musket balls the colonel had ordered each man to carry.

Sergeant Ford winked at Joel. "Private Benton all right, Captain?"

"All right, Nate. Let's see the rest of them."

After the inspection, they marched around the square

68

once in column, and then they fanned out in a long line and marched across the square abreast. They managed to stay in their relative positions fairly well, Joel decided. It might have been better to have tried it on a day when it wasn't so cold and windy, he thought. And then he remembered something the sergeant had said last night at supper. When it was time to fight, you could generally count on the weather being against you. It was either too hot or too cold or too wet or too dry. It seemed that there never was a good time to fight. Maybe there never was a good time to muster, either.

After the other two companies had marched around the square, they stood at attention on three sides while the captains went to where Doctor Tusten sat his horse. They saluted and the doctor and the officer beside him returned the salute.

"Look at the macaroni now," the man beside Joel muttered again. "He looks like he thinks he's queen of the May."

Joel grinned. The man did look pompous and self-important. There was a certain arrogance in the way he held his head, the supercilious way in which his hand flicked the return salute. He reminded Joel of someone who was trying hard to convince other people that he was something he wasn't.

The captains came back to their companies and spoke to the sergeants. Sergeant Ford turned to his company. "Company! Dis—missed!"

They made for the tavern at the end of the square on the run, as if there wouldn't be enough rum to go around.

Sergeant Ford came up to Joel. "Watch them run!" he chuckled. "Like a pack of fools."

Joel nodded absently. "Is it over for the day?"

"All over but the shouting, like they say."

"Well, I guess we'd better get back to the shop, then."

Sergeant Ford looked shocked. "Why, it's your holiday, boy. You probably want to study your books or something. Don't you?"

69

"Why, yes. I'd forgotten about the holiday."

"Well, you go right ahead and enjoy it. I want to go over there and see Joe Paxton about something. You tell the missus I might not find him before suppertime."

Sergeant Ford made off after the rest of the company as fast as he could travel.

The sergeant had not returned by suppertime, but Mrs. Ford was unperturbed. "It happens every muster day," she told Joel. "Nathan gets to thinking he's twenty years younger than he is, and then he manages to find somebody he can talk to about Rogers' Rangers and the Old French War."

Joel nodded politely and left Mrs. Ford to clear the dishes while he straightened the shop. It was always better to start the day with everything clean and tidy and in order. The day always seemed to go better, somehow.

By the time he was finished, Adam was knocking on the door for him to go along out to the Tusten home. He debated whether or not to take the musket Nathan Ford had loaned him. In the long run, it would be safer. There was no denying it.

"How was it?" Adam wanted to know.

"Well, we marched around the square and they inspected our arms. I guess that was about the long and the short of it."

Adam seemed mildly disappointed. "I watched some, but it got too cold standing there, and nobody seemed to be doing anything, so I went home."

"I guess that's the way it is in the army. Leastwise in the militia. You kind of stand around waiting and then when you do get around to doing something, it isn't very much anyway."

"Who was that officer with Doctor Tusten?"

"I don't know," Joel admitted. "He was from the Regulars, I guess. Because of his uniform."

Adam grinned. "I say that much and I'm not even in the militia."

Joel threw a friendly punch at Adam, who ducked dex-

70

terously and countered. "Come on," he said. "It's not going to get any warmer outside."

It was a good deal warmer in the Tusten kitchen than it had been on the road, Joel had to admit. The boys stood with their backs to the fire, letting the heat seep through their clothing and thaw the congealed blood.

The doctor grinned at them. "When you two scholars get your brains thawed out, come in the parlor and we'll get some work done." He rubbed his hands as if remembering the cold square and the men standing at attention.

As Joel followed Adam and the doctor into the parlor, he noticed with a sense of disappointment that Susan hadn't been there when he and Adam had come in. She was probably helping Mrs. Tusten put the children to bed early so that the lesson wouldn't be disturbed, he decided. He hoped she would be in the kitchen when they were ready to leave.

"Now, Adam," the doctor said. "Suppose you study this passage from Cicero, while Joel and I puzzle out some Caesar."

Joel felt a sense of relief. It had seemed to him that there was nothing to this Latin business but memorizing the various forms that had to be parsed or declined. The discipline of the language was what the doctor called it. Sometimes there seemed to be more discipline than language.

"Now, Joel," the doctor began. "When you go out in the woods hunting, what do you look for?"

Joel thought about it. "Well, first I find a sign."

"All right. And then what do you do about it?"

"Well, if it's a deer sign, I keep looking around for another one and I figure out which one's fresher. Then I keep going until I get on a trail I can follow."

"Very good," the doctor approved. "Now, reading a language can be like hunting. You pick up a sign, that's a word, and then you figure out whether it comes before or after another word. When you get enough of the signs together, you can make out the sense of it. That's the trail. Once you've got the trail, you can follow it until you get to the game.

That's the meaning. And the more trails you follow, the easier it gets. Just like going hunting."

Joel grinned. "I never thought about it that way."

"Most people don't," the doctor said drily. "They make such a business out of Latin that nobody wants to read it any more. Now tonight we're going to read some Caesar. He was a great soldier, and we can learn a few things from him that may help us against our own enemies."

The doctor opened the book and began to read, pronouncing the words slowly and carefully and holding the text so that Joel could see the words as he pronounced them. When he had finished the paragraph, he went back and read it in English, pointing out the words in Latin as he came to them.

"Now you try it," he said.

The first sentence was easy, because Joel had paid a good deal of attention to it. The others were a little harder, though. He had to think back over the words he had memorized before he could figure them out.

"Very good," the doctor said. "Now I'm going to give you this book to take with you. I want you to see how far you can get on your own. I'll just read you the next page the way I did before to get you started."

"That's a good way of doing it, sir," Joel said when the doctor had finished.

"Well," Doctor Tusten said modestly, "to tell you the truth, it's not original with me. A scholar of two hundred years ago first used this way of teaching. His name was Roger Ascham, and he was Queen Elizabeth's teacher. From all accounts, he did a good job with her."

Joel was impressed. It was something to know that you were being taught the same way a queen had been taught. It gave the language an extra measure of distinction, somehow.

"Now, Adam," the doctor said. "Let's see what you've been doing."

After the lesson, they went back into the kitchen. The doctor seemed as fresh as when they had started, Joel noticed. For his part, he felt as if half Caesar's army had been crawling through his head.

Mrs. Tusten was sitting before the fire and he felt a glow spread through him as he saw Susan bending down to get a kettle from the hanger in the fireplace. She looked up as they came in, and when he said good evening, she smiled shyly.

"I hope you boys can stay for a cup of tea and a cookie?" Mrs. Tusten said.

"Thank you, Mrs. Tusten," Adam said. "That would be very welcome after Cicero."

Joel smiled. "Thank you, ma'am. Caesar creates a hunger as well."

The doctor chuckled. "Anybody'd think you boys had been doing hard work. Wait until you get into Virgil."

Joel looked around the clean, bright room with its pewter gleaming in the firelight. Above the fireplace, the doctor's weapons hung on a rack. A rifle with a curly maple stock. A fowling piece and a musket. The blunderbuss Susan had held the night he had gone on the patrol with Sergeant Ford. Now they reminded him of something else.

"Doctor Tusten? Who was the officer that was with you today at the muster?"

"Oh, him." The doctor stretched out his feet to the fire. "He's Major Charles Morgan. Comes from one of the Regular Army units stationed over on the Hudson River. Colonel Hathorn sent him over to us to inspect our defenses. It seems that there's a rumor going around that we won't be able to count on the Regulars for help next summer. We're going to have to provide our own defense, and that means working together. If Minisink is attacked, for example, the Goshen militia will have to go to its aid. If we're attacked, Minisink and Lackawaxen and Big Eddy are supposed to come and help us."

"Oh," Joel said. "I thought I knew him from somewhere. He kind of looked familiar, but I couldn't place him."

The doctor looked at him. "Is the name at all familiar?"

Joel shook his head. "I never heard it before. I guess he just looked like somebody I knew once and forgot about. Maybe up at Edmeston."

"That often happens," the doctor smiled. "I once got ready to operate on a man for an ulcer on his left leg. When I got to the leg, there was no ulcer on it. He only looked like the man who had one."

"Why didn't he stop you? The wrong man, I mean?" Mrs. Tusten asked.

"I guess he couldn't pass up free medical attention," the doctor grinned. "Or maybe it was the glory of the thing."

Susan put down a plate with oatmeal cookies on it. Joel was very conscious of her clean, small hands and her freshly ironed gown. He was also conscious of the odor of train oil from his own hands. No matter how much you washed them, it seemed you could never quite get rid of the train oil. It was part of being a gunsmith, but he felt funny about it anyway.

Susan's hand came down once more and gave the plate half a turn. Now the largest of the cookies was in front of him. He felt his face reddening as he mumbled, "Thank you."

On the other side of the table, the doctor and his wife exchanged smiles.

EIGHT

JOEL'S arm felt better than it had all through the preceding week, despite the loading drill with the musket the day before. He decided that it wouldn't be long before it would be as good as new.

Sergeant Ford, on the other hand, looked decidedly ill. He had not returned from the tavern the evening before until long after Joel had returned from the doctor's house. He had probably had time to tell the story of his exploits with Rogers' Rangers several times over, Joel decided. If that was what rum did to you, it seemed like a good thing to stay away from.

"Do you feel all right, Mr. Ford?"

Nathan Ford cast a baleful glance at him. "I do not. I feel terrible."

"I'm sorry about that," Joel said, trying not to smile.

"It's not rum, if that's what you're thinking."

Joel let the smile come out. "As a matter of fact, that's what I was thinking."

Ford nodded. "I thought so. No, it's not rum. It's that new officer they've got. Major Charles Morgan. He came over to the tavern and stood some of us a round of drinks."

"Well, that should have made everybody happy," Joel said practically.

"Oh, well," Ford conceded. "Nobody turned down the drinks that I noticed. I stuck to ale, myself. It's safer."

"Well?"

Ford scratched his head. "It's hard to put your finger on any one thing. I guess it was the way he said things that

75

soured me on him. He kept talking like we had the whole war lost before we ever started. He was telling us that we didn't know the first thing about protecting ourselves. He said that the best way to do was to build a big fort and get inside it and stay there."

"What's wrong with that?"

Ford glared his exasperation. "Well, who in tarnation is going to feed all the people? The Army? Huh! They haven't got enough food themselves. We heard all about how the troops were starving down there in Pennsylvania last winter. At Valley Forge, I think it was."

"Well, that's only when the Indians come. The rest of the time, the farmers could be tending their cattle and their crops the same as always."

"Oh, no. That's not what Major Charles Morgan has in mind. He wants everybody to get together and build that fort and crawl in it and stay there. He said that as long as the farmers are planting and plowing and harvesting the Indians'll come. He said everybody who wants can go hunting, just as if there was enough game left to feed everybody."

"That doesn't sound very smart," Joel admitted.

"And another thing I didn't like. He said if we built a fort he only hoped it would be strong enough, because he heard where Butler and Brant are coming down with cannon next summer. Big ones they're going to haul overland on sledges."

"How in the world would anybody haul cannon through the woods? And if they did, where would they get enough powder to load them? It seems to me that you'd have to have a mighty big army to haul cannon around through the woods."

Ford nodded. "Sure you would. You can see that and I can see that. I tried to tell him, but he just looked at me and smiled like I was some kind of a bug or something, and he said that the British had ways of doing most anything they wanted to do. The thing is, Joel, it didn't bother me none, what he said. But a lot of the fellows in there, they ate it up, hook, line, and sinker. It scared the living daylights out of them."

Joel picked up a gunlock from the bench and looked at it. Cause and effect. You pulled the trigger, and the hammer fell. It was as simple as that. And as complicated. If everybody knew as much about mechanics as he and Sergeant Ford did, then everybody'd be a gunsmith. Maybe then everybody'd be able to see bad reasoning for what it was.

Ford growled to himself. "Then there was something else I didn't like. After he got all done telling us how to starve to death if the British didn't kill us with cannon first, then he told us that the Army is thinking about pulling out of York State entirely, come spring, and going off to fight in Connecticut or somewheres else. That way, we'd have the British army coming in from the east, the Indians from the west, and the Tories from all over. He might be right, at that."

"Well, he might be, but that's no sign we have to quit."

"No, it's not. But you take after that he started to tell about some of the places up north where they had had a lot of Indian raids. He said some of them had gone back to the King's side just to keep from being raided. Somebody asked him if they hadn't been raided anyway, and he said he hadn't heard, one way or the other."

"Well, maybe some of them have gone over to the British."

"It could be," Ford said. "But did he have to say so? And if he said they did, then he shouldn't have said it like he did."

"How was that?"

"Like he tried to scare us in the first place, telling us it was no use trying to farm. Then he told us even if we got in a fort it wouldn't do any good. And then he told us about

77

people who went over to the King's side and didn't get harmed."

"He didn't say that, did he? I thought he just said he hadn't heard."

"Well, he meant it, whether he said it or not."

Joel thought about it for a moment. Sergeant Ford was no man's fool, drunk or sober. If he thought there was something wrong with what the major had said, then there probably was. On the other hand, the doctor had met the major and talked with him. If there had been anything wrong, the doctor would have spotted it.

The trouble probably was that the major was an over-efficient, over-cautious blunderer. Regular soldiers might have overlooked his pessimism. The militia would take it seriously. Joel thought of Doctor Tusten, with his easy-going manner, his friendliness, and his quiet, direct way of giving orders. That was the sort of man the militia needed. Someone who didn't have to parade his superior knowledge to prove how good he was.

After breakfast, Mr. Ford came over to Joel. "Think you could tend the store for me?" he asked.

"Yes, sir."

"I have to go over to Minisink and put a lock on Jonas's store. He's got a lock, but he says it's not working right. Sometimes it won't close, and then again sometimes it won't open."

"That's no way for a lock to act."

Ford grinned. "It sure ain't."

"Do you want me to go? I could probably fix it all right."

"Do you feel up to it? I'd appreciate that. I could do it, but I don't mind saying I don't feel too much like going."

"No, I don't mind. I wanted to put a marker on Pa's grave anyway. I made me one out of that nice piece of walnut you gave me."

Mr. Ford looked relieved. "You go right ahead, then.

78

Take some oil and the little tool kit. If you can't fix it there, take it off and bring it back where we can look it over. You'd better take a hand axe to set the marker."

At first Joel thought of going straight to the claim, but he changed his mind when he got out of town. It was late and by the time he got to Minisink it would be later still. It would be noon by the time he got to Minisink and it could take him an hour or two to fix the lock. By the time he reached Goshen again, it would be black-dark, and he didn't know the way too well by night. On the other hand, he had come to Goshen from the claim several times and he knew that trail like the back of his hand.

The tools were safely tucked in his pouch, and he held the musket at the balance, where it carried easiest. He set a good swinging pace out of town along the wagon road, walking a hundred paces and then running the next hundred. A man could keep that up all day and never get tired.

Once he got out of sight of town, though, he left the road and took a short cut through the woods. It would slice three miles off the trip, and it was safer besides. There probably weren't any Indians around, but if there were they'd be watching the road to see if they could pick up a stray scalp.

Just as he had thought, the sun was almost directly overhead by the time he reached the stretch of wheatfield on the east side of the settlement.

Minisink looked as if it were well entrenched for the winter. The sawmill and the gristmill were both shut down, because the stream had frozen. Outside of a sleepy-looking sentry in the spy tower of Major Decker's palisade, there was no one in sight. He jogged up the empty street to Jonas's store.

Jonas was glad to see him. "Been wondering how you was making out, bub. How's the arm?"

79

"Pretty near as good as new. Another week or two and I won't even think about it. I noticed a lot of horse tracks in the woods. Who made them?"

"Oh, them. There's a Count Pulsomebody—Pulaski, that's it—and he's got a detachment of cavalry out to the west of us. We're supposed to feed him this winter."

"Who runs the stockade? Major Decker? Or the count?"

Jonas grinned. "The count runs the stockade now. Decker's got enough to do running his tavern, what with all the cavalry men being steady customers, even if they don't always pay." He changed the subject. "So you're working for Nate Ford. I can remember when Nate wouldn't let a soul get near his tools. Said they'd spoil them."

Joel grinned. "Maybe he was waiting for the right man."

Jonas winked the eye that was watching Joel. "Maybe he was. You think you can do something with the lock?"

"I don't know. Let's have a look."

He took the padlock over to the counter and examined it. It should be taken apart and cleaned, from the looks of it. He peered through the keyhole and saw traces of dirt and rust. "Don't you keep this oiled?" he asked.

"Nope," Jonas said proudly. "It only gets dirty faster when you keep oiling it all the time."

"What you can do," Joel said, "is to take a piece of wax or tallow and put it over the hole to keep the dirt out. Then you won't have to worry about oiling it."

"I never thought of that," Jonas admitted. "Can you fix it here?"

"If I can get the pins out, I can."

He unlocked the padlock to free the pins that held the two halves together and then he took the hammer and a small punch and the hand anvil he had brought with him and set to work. The pins drifted out without too much trouble and the mechanism of the lock was exposed. It seemed simple enough. The wards of the key struck pawls that ro-tated a notched bar which released or secured the notched

80

hasp. The pivots were not badly worn, but there was dirt and caked grease everywhere.

Jonas looked worried. He hovered over the lock as if to see what devil had possessed it.

Joel scraped away the caked dirt with the sharp end of a splinter of wood and then he carefully blew it out of the mechanism. A large ball of dust had collected near the pivot and it prevented the notched bar from engaging the hasp.

"That's all it was," he said. "Now we'll oil it and see what happens."

The lock clicked quite happily, and Joel put the halves together and drifted the pins into place, setting them by spreading the ends slightly with the hammer and the punch.

"I'll be switched," Jonas said with amazement. "Just as good as Nate could have done it. How much do I owe?"

"Mr. Ford said it would be a shilling."

Jonas looked surprised. "That's a lot of money."

"Well, Mr. Ford said since I had to come over here to fix it, it ought to cost more."

Jonas grinned to show him there were no hard feelings. "I was just trying it on for size, you might say. It didn't fit, but there's no harm trying."

"None at all," Joel smiled.

Jonas fished in his strongbox for the shilling. "You see any Indian sign out there?" he asked.

"Not a thing. The woods are bare. There isn't much game, either. Not even deer."

"That's what the major said."

"Who?"

"That new officer, Major Morgan. He rode over this morning to see what the stockade looked like. Said the Army had sent him around to find out how good the militia defenses were."

So the major had got around to looking at Minisink, too. "I hope he liked what he saw," Joel said drily.

"Oh, he told us we'd be all right if we pulled everybody

into the stockade come spring. Unless the British haul in cannon, that is. If they do that, nobody'll be safe." Jonas cocked a shrewd right eye at Joel. "Sounds to me like you don't think much of the major."

"I don't know him," Joel said. "But Sergeant Ford was telling me that he had scared some of the farmers over in the tavern yesterday, telling them about the cannon and all the rest of it."

"Well, he's the one who ought to know about those things. Ain't that right?"

"I guess it is," Joel conceded. "Well, I'd better be heading back. I want to stop by the claim and put a marker on Pa's grave."

Jonas looked sympathetic. "I didn't see a lot of your Pa the last year, but I miss him all the same." He blew his nose lustily. "How's your arm after all that hammering?"

"Fine. You see, the ball didn't go in very deep. I guess it must have been a long-range shot."

"You were lucky. Try to keep on being lucky; hear?"

Joel grinned and shook hands with Jonas. "I'll work on it," he promised.

He followed the same path that he had followed that other afternoon in November, across the wheatfields and up the ridge on the other side. He wasn't thinking about that afternoon as much as he was thinking about the next afternoon, when he had gone out with Sergeant Ford's patrol. Now he remembered how they had stopped on the ridge just across the creek from the house and waited while the others went down to dig a grave. In his mind's eye he could see the sunlight flashing from the blade of the hand axe as the man worked away behind the chimney. And then another image appeared. The image of a footprint made by a heavy-soled Army boot on the melting snow that covered the ice of the creek.

He shook his head impatiently. This was no way to be traveling through the woods. When you were in the woods, you ought to be paying attention to the things that were going on around you, not daydreaming.

At the top of the ridge he stopped and looked back at the village. It was easy to see against the snow-covered background, with its attendant spirals of smoke soiling the clear blue of the sky. It was easy to see his footprints, too. If anybody had wanted to trail him, he had left tracks that a child could follow. He looked back down the slope, watching the rock outcroppings carefully for signs of movement. There were none. Satisfied, he turned back to the descent of the ridge.

The creek was frozen over, and he made good time crossing it and climbing the ridge on the far side. He kept up a sort of jogtrot, partly to save time, and partly to get warm again. He had felt the cold come up from the ground into his feet the minute he had stopped back there. Perhaps when he got to the claim he would stop and make a fire. It would be a long, cold trudge back to Goshen and there was nothing like starting out warm. If he didn't take too much time now, he'd probably have time to make a fire when he got to the claim.

At the place where he had discarded his bundle that other afternoon, he paused to look for the deerskin fragment that had been caught in the branches of a tree, but it was gone now. Gone, too, were the footprints of Sergeant Ford's patrol; subsequent snows had covered all trace of the two days in November.

Just short of the crest of the ridge he stopped and looked behind him once more. The trail was still empty.

And then he was at the top and the creek lay below him, and the cornfield beyond that, the withered stalks barely projecting above the frozen crust of the snow. And beyond the field were the blackened logs that had once been his home.

He stood still for a moment, his head just showing over

the crest, holding his musket in both hands, now, ready to use. But the clearing was empty. The snow lay virginal and unbroken in a carpet extending from the creek to the far line of trees. Or did it? There seemed to be a track of some sort at one corner of the clearing. Footprints would hardly be visible at this distance; the snow was frozen too hard to take that sharp an imprint. What had made the tracks?

He looked carefully along the ridge behind where the house had stood. Nothing moved. As far as he could tell, there was no other living thing within a mile of him.

All right, he told himself. Stop getting jumpy. Just go on down there and find out what made the tracks and stop worrying about them.

As he came across the cornfield, he took a wide cast to the south so that he could come up on the chimney from the side. If anything were hiding behind it, he would be able to see it before he was too close to retreat. He kept the musket ready until he had circled the ruins of the cabin and seen the second set of tracks leading away. A horse had made them. A horse shod with fairly new shoes, judging from the sharpness of the prints. The weight of the animal and rider had been enough to leave relatively deep prints, even on the hard-frozen crust.

He wondered what the rider had been doing here. Anyone could see from a distance that the fire had been hot enough to destroy everything worth having. Everything except the iron kettle and the frying pan, anyhow.

Joel walked across a fallen log, half-consumed, that projected above the surface of the snow. The kettle and the pan were still on the hearth where they belonged. No one could help but see them, yet no one had taken them. What had the rider wanted?

He put it out of his mind. It was getting late and he had to get the marker put in. That could be a job and a half. He walked around the cabin to the grave mound behind the chimney. The men of Ford's patrol had carefully covered the mound with rocks from the foundation, and some of them stuck out of the snow.

He looked at the mound and sudden tears burned at his eyes. It's so cold out here, he thought. Pa always liked the fire, and it's so cold out here. But that was foolish. It didn't matter to Pa, where he was. What was here, that was only the body a person used while he was on earth. The part that really counted was the spirit, like Parson Hanley said. And as long as you remembered a person, it was almost like having him with you. The thing to do was not to think about something that didn't matter, but to think about the things Pa had taught him, the way he had always been patient, no matter how many mistakes he had made. Every time he went in the woods, he thought about how Pa had taught him to track game, how to tell the print of a wolf, how to find a honey tree. In a way, it was like having Pa there.

Joel leaned the musket against the chimney within easy reach and freed the axe from his belt. He began to chop at the snow with quick, light strokes, so as not to hit a rock. When he got down to dirt, the frozen grains spilled over the snow in a warm brown cascade. He put the axe down and scooped out snow and dirt with his hands until he had the hole cleared. Then he stood up and took the musket and walked around the cabin to see if the noise of the axe had attracted anything.

Satisfied that it had not, he returned to the grave and deepened the hole until his elbow was just above the level of the ground when he reached down into the hole. Only about a foot of the marker would be above ground level, but it would be enough for now. Some day, he would get a nice flat piece of limestone and cut a regular marker. But for now, this would have to do.

It looked pretty good, even if he did say so himself. The walnut had been donated by Nathan Ford from a supply he kept for musket stocks. It had been treated by boiling in oil so that it would resist damp and rot. Joel had smoothed

85

it and shaped it with a draw-knife and pumice until it was like glass, and he had cut Pa's name with one of Nathan Ford's cold chisels. The letters were deep and they stood out nicely. The only trouble was, they looked square, like the blade of the chisel.

He placed the marker in the hole, resting it on a bed of pebbles so that the water would drain quickly away, and then he tamped the earth back in place along the ends and sides, using the back of the axe to pound it down solidly.

Finally he stood up and fastened the axe to his belt. It was a job he had been wanting to do ever since the day the patrol had come to bury Pa, but here it was almost the beginning of January already. He picked up his musket and stood there for a moment, awkwardly. Part of him wanted to stay because it was the thing you were probably supposed to do, but part of him was saying it was late already and he'd have to make tracks to get through the woods to the road before it got dark. There wouldn't be a moon tonight, either.

"Goodbye, Pa," he said. And then he turned away.

When he left the clearing, he followed the horse's track because it was headed in the right direction and because it was easy to see how deep the snow was, just in case there were any soft places where he might fall through. The track led all the way to the road. He could feel the indentations through his moccasins, even after it got dark.

He wondered what the rider had wanted to look at in a burned-out log house. He decided that maybe he'd mention it to the doctor when he went for his next lesson.

NINE

IT was almost a week before Joel got a chance to see the doctor. He and Adam had studied together the evening before, and Adam had complained that he had missed hunting with Joel, since Joel had gone to Minisink to fix Jonas' lock instead.

"Everything seems more exciting in the woods," Adam said. "You always have the feeling that something has just happened or that something is just about to happen."

"Well, nothing just had and nothing did," Joel chuckled.

"Did you put up the marker on your father's grave?" Joel nodded. "It looked good."

"I'll bet it did. Wasn't that exciting?"

"I guess so, if that's what you call exciting." And then he remembered the hoofprints on the snow. He told Adam.

"Well!" Adam exclaimed. "What did Mr. Ford say about that?"

"I didn't tell him," Joel admitted. "To tell the truth, it kind of slipped my mind."

"It's mysterious," Adam went on, his eyes dancing with excitement. "Let's tell the doctor about it tomorrow night. I'll bet he'll be interested."

The next night after they had finished their Latin and gone to the kitchen for cookies and sassafras tea, Joel mentioned the matter.

The doctor listened with grave courtesy. "I imagine it was Major Morgan," he said when Joel had finished. "If he was over to Minisink, he could have stopped off on his

87

way back here. The major has been familiarizing himself with the country around here so that he can offer us advice."

"If he's going to advise us how to defend ourselves, sir," Adam protested, "it seems to me that he wouldn't be bothered with a burned-out log house."

"Well, Adam, sometimes a man does things that aren't always as sensible as they might be." The doctor sipped at his tea. "Let's say whoever it was was being curious and let it go at that."

"Why did they send the major to help us with our defense, sir?" Joel asked.

"Well, Joel. That's a long story."

Susan smiled at Joel, and he met her glance without his usual confusion. It surprised him so much that he forgot to avoid her eyes. Instead he smiled back.

"There's a rumor going around," the doctor continued. "I've heard it from the major and from Colonel Hathorn as well. It seems that General Sullivan has been ordered to fit out an expedition against the Indian villages to the west. Most of the Tory and Indian raids have come by way of Unadilla. It's one of the biggest of the Indian towns, and it's located in a strategic spot, right at the confluence of Unadilla River and the Susquehanna. You see, the raiders coming down from Canada can stop off there for food and rest before they make their raids."

Mrs. Tusten leaned forward in her chair and refilled the doctor's cup. "It's going to be a long story," she murmured parenthetically, and her eyes crinkled with laughter.

"At any rate, Congress feels that if the Army raids the Indian villages and drives the Indians out, the Tories won't be able to use them as advance bases for their raids on us. They'll have to come all the way from Canada without having a place to rest and refit, and they'll be unable to send as many men as they have in the past."

"General Burgoyne managed to send a whole army down to fight us," Joel said. "And he didn't get beaten because he didn't have help. He got beaten because he wasn't a good soldier."

Doctor Tusten grinned. "That is an understatement. Burgoyne was no kind of soldier at all, good or bad. But the rest of it is perfectly true. Sullivan can destroy the Indian towns. I have no doubt of his ability to do so. But it's not going to solve our problems at all. You see, the point is not how many towns you can capture, but how many of the enemy you can defeat. We're not interested in fighting towns. After all, no town ever fought me or anyone else. It's men who do the fighting, and if the men escape from the towns, as they're sure to do, we'll still have them to reckon with."

"That sounds sensible, Uncle Ben," Susan said quietly. "Why don't they send us some of the soldiers instead?"

"That's a good question," the doctor said wryly. "For the same reason that they have consistently cheated the Indians out of their land. They're short-sighted and greedy."

"How could the Indians have stayed here after the settlers moved in?" Joel asked.

"That goes back about fifty years. We chased the Delawares off their land without proper negotiation or compensation. They resented it, but they went. When the Iroquois nation took over the Indian affairs of this part of the country, they demanded a reckoning, but all they got was talk. We finally made some sort of token payment, but it wasn't enough, and it was too late. There was a great deal of resentment, and when we did the same thing at the beginning of the Revolution, they went over to the British. We sent men who were too stupid and prejudiced to come to any sort of agreement with anybody. And besides, our commissioners weren't empowered to sign any sort of treaty with the Iroquois. They were supposed to talk to them and keep them peaceful. Some of the commissioners had been cheating those same Indians for years. That was their sole qualification!"

The doctor's eyes were shining with anger, now. "There was a settlement of Conestoga Indians down in the Wyoming

Valley. They had become Christian and built houses and started to farm. They went to church and got on well with their white neighbors. And then the Connecticuters came in and burned them out and killed as many as they could, saying that it was their land and that Pennsylvania had no right to give it to Indians or whites, either one. When an Indian takes a good, long look at white-man justice, it's no wonder that he doesn't trust us. Most of the Indians would have been willing to share with us. We had different customs, but they were willing to adopt them. We had guns and clothing and farming methods and a written language to offer in exchange for some of their land. After all, we must remember that the Danes and Angles settled side by side in old England. Not to mention the Saxons and the Normans, later on. There was violence and friction, yes. But eventually there was peace and a merging of the peoples. Here? All the average white settler wants is to exterminate the Indian completely and try to justify it because they're 'heathen.' "

"And they want to exterminate us in turn," Joel said. "Is it always going to be this way?"

"I don't know," the doctor said. "I suppose it starts when the people who don't quite fit in a civilized society —the law-breakers, the criminal element—find themselves in trouble with the law, and go to the frontier where the law enforcement is practically nil. They break the treaties at will and get the Indians provoked to attack. Then the commissioners blame the Indians. As long as we can't enforce our treaties on our own people, this will continue."

Joel nodded. Somehow, being an Indian fighter didn't sound like much, in the face of the doctor's discussion. It was one thing to fight hard when you had right on your side. It was quite another thing to fight people who probably had families just like your own. He realized suddenly that whenever he had thought of Indians, he always had thought of warriors. But the warriors had to have fathers and mothers. They had to be married and have children, just the same as

90

the whites did. It was a puzzler, and if it were all the way the doctor said it was, then General Sullivan and his army weren't going to do a lot of good.

As he and Adam walked home in the clear, cold night, Joel thought about the doctor and his grasp of politics, of military strategy, and of life in general. He was what you might call a well-rounded man.

"He looks at life in one piece," he said to Adam. "Some men just see their own side of things. They're doctors or lawyers or whatever, and that's all they can see. Take Mr. Ford, for example. He's a good gunsmith and a good ranger, but he doesn't know or care what's going on up in Albany or down in Congress."

Adam chuckled. "That's the difference between a good man and a great one. And the best thing of all is the way Doctor Tusten stayed on here to help keep people well. He could have gone to Congress if he had wanted anything out of it for himself. But he doesn't. He just wants to be useful. I don't know of anybody else like that, except my father, and he has to be. That's part of being a minister of God."

"Well," Joel said. "I don't know as I'd want to be a minister. I want to be a doctor. But I do know this much; I want to try to be the kind of doctor that Doctor Tusten is. If you're only going to work for yourself, it seems to me you're missing one of the biggest parts of life."

Adam changed the subject. "I wish he had thought more about the rider who went down to your claim."

Joel laughed. "I think you just want to go out there and see for yourself. Isn't that it?"

"Well, I guess maybe it is. I haven't been more than three or four miles outside of town on any of our hunts."

"All right," Joel promised. "Next time we go out we'll strike out in that direction."

Before he went to bed that night, Joel went over to

the fire and looked at his arm. There was a little red indentation with white scar tissue radiating from it, but it had healed clean. A lot of wounds didn't. He wondered whether he could have done as good a job of taking out the ball as had the doctor. Maybe it wasn't only skill. Maybe it was practice, as well. He had once cut a buckshot out of a neighbor's leg when Pa had been gone from home and there was no one else to do it, but there was quite a difference in size between a buckshot and a musket ball. Still, with the doctor teaching him, he ought to be able to do it. He had a good steady hand, and people seemed to think he had common sense.

Common sense told him that he had a long way to go before he could be a doctor. Maybe he would never make it, but if he didn't, it wouldn't be for lack of trying. Maybe he would just go back to the claim and build a new cabin and make a living hunting and trapping. No. That was doing for yourself, not adding to anyone else's life. A man ought to help other men. He ought to help his wife, too, and she would help him in turn.

And then he thought about Susan.

A week later, he had forgotten all about his promise to Adam until they started out of town and Adam reminded him.

"It's pretty near seven miles," he warned Adam.

"I can make it easy."

"Besides, the hunting is just as good closer to town. Or just as bad, depending on how you look at it."

Adam grinned. "I don't care. You didn't see the place like a stranger would have seen it, so you wouldn't be thinking the way that rider was thinking. I want to see if I can figure out just what was on his mind."

It was good and cold, for which Joel was thankful. It made walking a whole lot easier and they wouldn't leave

92

any trail worth following. They made good time as a result, and they struck the ridge behind the claim well before noon. He halted Adam while he looked across the clearing to the cornfield and to the creek beyond.

Snow had drifted over the hoofprints for the most part, although he could make them out at the very edge of the clearing where the wind had scoured them clean. There were no other tracks that he could see, but that didn't mean much. It was too cold for anything lighter than a horse and rider to break the crust.

"I'm going down and circle the place," he told Adam. "You stay up here and cover me. When it's all right to come down, I'll wave."

He went down the slope fairly fast and trotted around the edge of the clearing, far enough from the house so that no one hiding behind the chimney could jump him. But there was no one there. He knew that he would have taken the precaution in any event, but it was also true that Adam had got him worked up over the hoofprints. Adam had quite an imagination when you got right down to it.

At the crest of the ridge Adam was leaning on his father's fowling piece. He waved and then Adam waved back and came down the slope. He was practically running by the time he hit the level ground, and he began to caper and cavort as he made his way to Joel. His mouth opened for a yell, but Joel looked sternly at him.

"We keep quiet in the woods."

Adam flushed and looked down at his boots. "I forgot."

Joel gave him a friendly punch on the arm and smiled. "We do that, too, sometimes. The thing is, if you fool around, pretty soon you'll make a lot of noise. The least thing that can happen is you'll scare the game. The worst thing is that you'll draw Indians."

"Does it matter, if there are Indians out?"

Joel nodded. "This is a bad spot to get caught. It's open ground to the creek or the ridge, either one. There's

93

no good place to hide and shoot it out. You could get behind the chimney or lie behind one of the logs, but it's hard to reload and they could come up behind you."

"Oh."

Joel grinned. "Let's forget it. Did you figure out what the rider was doing here?"

"I don't know. I guess he was just looking at the chimney. It's about the only thing left standing. Maybe he wanted to see what was holding it up."

"Could be."

Behind the chimney, the grave marker stood out above the snow, a rich warm brown. It looked fine. He walked over to it and stood there for a moment with his cap off. Adam came up beside him and took off his cap, too.

"It looks nice," Adam said finally. "You did a good job on it, Joel."

He nodded. It was funny the way you thought about solemn things off in the woods, but here and now he was only thinking that it was cold and that they had better start back and see about shooting something. He put on his cap and turned away from the grave. Adam followed him.

They walked around the chimney and then he remembered. Pa had kept some money hidden in a leather pouch under one of the hearth stones. One way or another, he had forgotten all about it.

"What's the matter?" Adam wanted to know.

"Pa kept his money under one of the hearth stones," he said. "I think maybe I ought to get it, as long as we're out here."

He dug away snow and ashes with a piece of charred sapling that had fallen in from the roof until he recognized the stone. It had quartz in it, or mica, and it glistened in the sun as he turned it over.

The bag was intact, but the leather had become soaked with snow that had melted and frozen since the fire had left the hearth open to the elements. He put it in his pouch.

When he got back to the Ford house, he could thaw it out and dry it.

"What's that?" Adam asked curiously.

"What's what?"

"That string hanging out of the chimney."

A length of leather thong dangled just below the level of the top of the fireplace. A man standing up wouldn't have been able to see it. He pulled at it. It was solid.

Adam stuck his head in the fireplace opening and looked up. "It's awful big, Joel, whatever it is."

"Let's have a look."

He reached up and felt a fairly thick bundle wrapped in leather. When he looked up into the chimney, he could see that the bundle was about five feet long. It had been thrust up into the chimney so that the top rested on one wall of the chimney while the bottom balanced on a rock projecting from the other wall. He pushed up on the bottom and freed it, and then the weight of it bore him down. He just managed to get his hands out of the way before it crashed onto the stones of the hearth.

"Well, that's a puzzler," Adam said. "Is it yours?"

He shook his head. "Not Pa's, either. Pa had his surveying instruments wrapped up, but they took those when they burned the cabin. We found where they had broken them up the next day, when I came out with Mr. Ford."

"Let's open it, then."

The thong was knotted loosely enough and he worked the knot out with his bare hands. Before he opened the wrapping, he put his mittens on again.

Adam gave an exclamation as the bundle was opened. There were five muskets inside. Each of them was heavily coated with thick grease, apparently to protect them from the weather. They were new, judging from the absence of scratches on the barrels and the stocks, and they bore the King's mark on the lock-plates. Five small pouches wrapped with them contained fifty cartridges apiece.

Adam picked up one of the cartridges. "What's this?"

"It's a new way of loading. The British have been using it. You tear the paper and the powder and ball are inside. After you pour the powder down the muzzle, you wad the paper and then you put the ball in last. That way, you don't have to stop and measure out powder."

"Pretty smart, I'd say. What in the world is all this stuff doing here?"

"I don't know. There aren't any British around that I know about. Maybe it's something the militia is storing here."

"Wouldn't you have heard about it?" Adam asked.

"I don't know. Maybe it's something only the doctor knows about. I guess the thing to do is put it all back the way we found it and tell him."

Adam nodded approval. "I'd like to know if this had anything to do with the rider who came in here. Did he get off his horse?"

Joel thought about it. "Yes, he did. There were footprints all around where the snow wasn't too frozen to take them. Maybe it had something to do with the new defense plan."

He retied the bundle carefully and poked the barrel end upward. As it scraped along the wall of the chimney, a shower of soot cascaded down onto the hearth. Suddenly, a leather pouch fell to the hearth with a plop.

Adam turned it over. It was secured with a hasp and a padlock. "I guess we can't open that," he said ruefully.

Joel grinned. "Haven't you had enough excitement for one day?" he asked. He picked up the pouch and reached up into the chimney until he found the ledge of rock where the pouch had rested. Then he balanced the bundle containing the muskets so that it was as it had been before.

"Let's turn up some of these hearth stones," he told Adam.

"What do you want to do that for?"

"It's too late to keep anybody from knowing we've been

here. All that soot is a giveaway. But if we say we came looking for Pa's money, we have a good excuse. And the dirt under the stones will hide the soot. I don't want anybody to know we found the muskets until we tell the doctor."

Adam's mouth opened in a round "O" of surprise. "What do you think it means?"

Joel turned it over in his mind. "Probably nothing bad," he said finally. "It probably means that the doctor wants some weapons outside the stockade, so that if the place is overrun and there are survivors, they won't be unarmed. But it could mean Tory spies, too. Until we find out for sure, let's not go talking about it. All right?"

Adam nodded. He was too excited to talk.

TEN

A relatively light snowfall during the winter had left the woods open. Consequently, the deer didn't herd the way they usually did, and hunting became increasingly difficult. Search as he might, Joel could find no deer tracks on the way back from the claim. The best he and Adam could do was to bring down a rabbit. It was not even a good-sized rabbit, and it was hardly worth the powder and shot it took to get it.

By the time they reached the outskirts of Goshen, it was beginning to get dark. Adam headed for home, after arranging to pick Joel up on his way to the Tusten house that evening.

Nathan Ford looked quizzically at the rabbit. "It's a mighty small git you've got," he said ruefully. "I guess you didn't have a lot of work carrying it."

"Well," Joel smiled, "I've got more than a rabbit, only I couldn't carry it all."

"What is it?"

"Adam and I kind of made up that we wouldn't talk about it until we talked to the doctor. Do you think you could come along with us?"

"What's it about, boy?"

"Well, sir, I guess you'd call it militia business."

Ford nodded. "In that case, I guess I'll have to come along. Can't you tell me about it first?"

"I would," Joel said, "but I told Adam not to talk to anybody until we had seen the colonel, so it wouldn't be right for me to, either."

"All right. I'll come along a little later, after you boys get done with your lessons."

But when Joel and Adam reached the Tusten house, they saw a horse tied to the big maple near the back door.

"Looks like the doctor has company," Adam said.

"Well, we'll just go in and work on our lessons. Don't say anything in front of whoever it is."

"All right," Adam agreed.

Susan opened the door for them and put her finger to her lips. "Uncle Ben is talking with Captain Brown and Major Morgan. He said to start on your lessons in here and he'd see you when he got done."

Joel smiled at her. "I guess that's what we'll have to do, then. We wanted to see the doctor about something else, but that can wait, too."

From the inner room they could hear the rise and fall of voices, and try as he might Joel could not concentrate upon his translation for the excitement of his and Adam's discovery.

The three men were apparently discussing the defense plans of the county. Major Morgan was emphasizing the gravity of the situation. The Indians would come early this year, because the woods were relatively free of snow and the ground would dry out fast, once the April sun got to it.

Captain Brown broke in to say that he had heard all that before, and that he wished they would concentrate on fighting the Indians instead of running away from them. The major cut in on him with his supercilious drawl. It was fine to be brave, he said, but first you had to stay alive.

Joel found himself wondering why Doctor Tusten had nothing to say. The major was suggesting that the Minisink people might come over to Goshen, if they couldn't hold their stockade, and still the doctor said nothing. The major went on to say that it was going to be a hard summer and an even harder winter to follow, and then Captain Brown cut in again to say that some people could talk themselves into losing a fight before the fight ever got a chance to start.

100

"How far have you gone?" Susan asked quietly.

"I haven't," Joel admitted. "I can't seem to get my mind off what they're talking about."

"Well," Susan said tartly. "You won't get to be a doctor that way."

"I guess not," Joel admitted.

"Read some to me?"

He nodded and she drew up a chair beside him. He read slowly, pointing to the words as he went, and then translating them. Susan's head bent close to his own, and he was very conscious of her. If the Indians came, he would want to be here where he could protect her. He saw himself firing through the window at a Tory, the Tory with the black leather cap and the white cockade, while behind him Susan loaded a spare musket.

"What is 'Helvetii'?" Susan asked. "You skipped that one."

"Swiss," he said, flushing. "I guess I wasn't thinking about it, just then."

Across the table, Adam grinned knowingly. Drat him, Joel thought.

Abruptly, the door opened and the three men walked out.

"Doing a little teaching, Joel?" the doctor smiled.

"In a way, sir. I was reading some of my lesson to Susan."

"The best way in the world to learn," the doctor approved. "I'll be with you boys in a moment."

As they walked through the kitchen, the three men were smiling as if they had suddenly composed their differences. Joel realized that they had sensed the nearness between Susan and himself.

In a moment the doctor reappeared with Nathan Ford in tow. Outside, the major's horse clattered on the frozen ground where the wind had swept away the snow.

"Nathan says you have something to tell me," the doctor said. "Militia business?"

101

"Yes, sir."

"Perhaps you should have mentioned it earlier, while Major Morgan and Captain Brown were here. If there were anything to be done, they would have to know about it."

Joel cleared his throat. "Well, sir. It was something I wanted you to hear alone, first. With Sergeant Ford, that is. Maybe it's all right for everybody to know, but maybe it isn't. I didn't want to take chances on the wrong people hearing it.

"Quite right," Doctor Tusten approved. "It never hurts to be careful."

"We went out to Pa's claim today, because Adam wanted to know what that horseman had been doing there a couple of weeks ago. I told Sergeant Ford about it, right after I told you. You said it had probably been the major inspecting defenses."

Doctor Tusten's face changed very slightly. Behind the pleasant exterior, the colonel of the Goshen militia made his appearance. "Yes?"

"When we got there today, we—I mean Adam—saw a thong hanging out of the fireplace. When we looked, we found a bundle wrapped up in a cowhide. I opened it and found five brand-new Brown Bess muskets and five brand-new cartridge pouches with cartridges in them."

"What!" Doctor Tusten barked. "Where are they?"

"We put them back, sir. I didn't know whether it was something the militia had left or not, so I put them back the way they were. There was a leather pouch, too, but I couldn't see what was in it because it had a padlock on it."

Nathan Ford's lips tightened. "I told you, Doc. There's plenty of Tories still around here."

The doctor nodded. "I know it, Nate. The thing is, what to do about the muskets?"

"Go get them."

"I guess you're right. I was thinking of setting a trap to catch the man who put them there, but we might have to wait a month." He turned to Joel. "You said there was a pouch, as well?"

"Yes, sir."

"I wish I knew what was in that pouch." The doctor frowned. "Nate, can Joel go hunting again tomorrow?"

"Sure he can. He only got a snowshoe rabbit today, so nobody'd think anything of it. Want me to go?"

"No. I don't want anybody to know about this. I want you two boys to leave before dawn and get out there. Pick up the muskets and the pouch and bring them in. You can have my horse, if you like."

Joel shook his head. "If we don't take our own guns, we can carry the muskets out. A horse might look suspicious, if anybody saw us. More so than seeing us unarmed."

"I still think I ought to go along, Doc," Nathan Ford protested. "If a Tory put those muskets there, he might be watching the place."

"I know," Doctor Tusten said. "But that's a chance we'll have to take. If you went, your absence might be noted by the wrong people, and then there'd be the devil and all to pay." He turned to Joel. "If you meet anybody, you were just going out to see your father's grave. You'll have to say you were careless and left your muskets home. If you don't meet anyone, get down there and load two of the muskets as quickly as you can. Get the muskets and the pouch, and get out of there fast. The longer you stay near the claim, the more chance there'll be of someone spotting you."

Joel nodded. "Yes, sir."

Across the room he saw Susan looking at him with something like admiration in her eyes. Suddenly he felt about ten feet tall.

Even though they had started out early, it was light long before they left the road. Joel set a fast pace that forced Adam to a trot. From the looks of the morning, the day was going to be warm and bright. That meant that the snow would be melting in the sunny places and that they would leave tracks. There wasn't much anybody could do about it, but if

103

they could get into the woods where the trees shaded the snow, they would be able to hide their trail pretty well there. The trick was to leave the road before the snow melted enough to take prints that would show that they had left it.

At a point where a rock outcropping came down to the road, Joel turned off, jumping from the edge of the road on to a rock so that he would not leave prints. He watched approvingly as Adam followed him.

"All right?" Adam asked.

"Fine. Now let's make some miles."

The going was easy in the woods. There wasn't too much snow, and what there was was still frozen fairly hard. If you went at a trot and didn't put your feet down hard, you could stay on top of it without any trouble.

As nearly as he could judge, it was ten o'clock by the time they reached the ridge that overlooked the clearing. Joel held up his hand for a halt.

"We'll stop and rest for a little while here," he said. "Once we get down there, we're going to have to move fast, so we might as well have all our strength about us."

"And wits?" Adam grinned.

"And wits. Can you carry two muskets?"

Adam nodded proudly. "Easy as pie. I could take three, if I had to."

Joel threw a mock punch at him. "Quit boasting. You'll wish you'd never found those muskets by the time we get back."

"No, I won't. How about if I load two and carry them while you take the other three on your back? Then I can hand you one, if we get chased."

"All right. That sounds fine." He looked across the clearing at the creek and at the ridge across from it. It seemed peaceful enough. If there had been anyone lurking on the other side, there probably would have been birds flying around. But supposing there weren't any birds? He made up his mind.

"You go around to the north until you're level with

the chimney. Keep your eyes open and see if you can spot anything where the hill slopes down to the creek. I'll do the same thing on the south. When you get level with the chimney, come on down into the clearing and meet me, unless you hear something."

"What would I hear?"

"You'd hear me running for Goshen like thunder, for one thing. Come on, let's get started."

As soon as Joel had seen Adam safely started, he looked back down the ridge in the direction from which they had come. The back trail showed no sign of life, but he felt nervous anyhow. The other day he had not known about the muskets. Maybe they hadn't been there then. He had come down and put the marker over Pa's grave and gone home, and there was nothing special to worry about. Even yesterday, when he had come with Adam, there had been nothing special to worry about at first. But now that he knew there was a good reason for someone to be watching the clearing, there was a lot to worry about.

The south end of the ridge was empty. He zig-zagged in the timber to make sure that it was safe and then he turned down towards the clearing in time to see Adam break free of the timber on the opposite side. He waved at Adam and Adam waved back at him. Everything was fine, so far.

"Nothing up there," Adam announced proudly, as they met at the chimney.

"Good. Let's move."

He reached up the chimney and dislodged the bundle. This time, he made no effort to conceal the fact that he had been here. He laid the muskets on the ground and untied the thong. The sun glinted on the bright metal of the barrels and the locks.

"Start loading," he told Adam. "I want to get that pouch."

He peered up the chimney cautiously, in order to stay as clean as he could. The pouch was still on the tiny ledge where he had left it. He reached up and grabbed it by one corner of the flap. It had no carrying straps, so he thrust it into his hunting pouch for easy carrying.

"Here's one," Adam said.

"All right. Load another while I tie the rest of them together."

Adam's ramrod rattled busily as he tamped down the charge. Joel watched him for a moment, and then he took the thong which had tied the bundle together and fastened the three remaining muskets with three turns around the barrels and another three turns through the trigger guards. Then he took the cowhide that the muskets had been wrapped in and cut two wide strips. He knotted these together at one end and passed the other end through the trigger guards until the knot jammed. Satisfied, he stood up and took the weight of the muskets by passing the strap over his right shoulder, across his chest, under his left armpit, and over his left shoulder. He grasped the end of the strap with his left hand and stamped once or twice to get the play out of the strap.

Adam chuckled. "You look like a one-man army."

"What's worse, I feel like one. Are you ready?"

"I'm fine. How about the pouches?"

"Can you handle three of them? I can take two if you put the straps over the butts of the muskets."

Adam looped the straps over the musket butts, and then he strapped on the remaining pouches, one over each shoulder and one around his neck.

"They weigh more than I figured," he said. "I never knew they could get that heavy."

"Wait a while," Joel counseled. "They'll get heavier."

"Huh! Let's get started."

"Not that way," Joel said. "Head for the creek."

Adam stared at him. "It's longer that way."

"Not much, and it's a whole lot safer. We'll be under cover until we get to the other side of the ridge."

"But there's nobody up there," Adam protested.

106

"There wasn't when we were up there. You don't know what's up there now."

Obediently, Adam trotted after him in the direction of the creek.

He took the most direct route, not bothering about making tracks now. The important thing was to save time. It would take a fool or a desperate man to attack two men with five muskets, once they had reached the shelter of the creek. We could pretty near stand off an army, he thought proudly.

The cornfield extended right up the slope to the base of the ridge which curved horseshoe-fashion around the clearing. It was perhaps a hundred yards from the ruins of the house to the nearest cover, the point at which the creek lapped the base of the ridge. The man who had built the house originally had cleared a good deal of land, partly for farming purposes, and partly to deny cover to marauding Indians. The only thing vulnerable about the position of the house was the commanding position of the ridge. That had been outweighed by the value of having the house down near the water and concealed from view, except from the ridge itself.

They trotted past the path that led directly to the creek and headed for the place where the ridge fell off to the creek bed. It would be easy traveling, once they got on the ice, Joel thought. It might be a little longer, but it would be easier. Loaded down the way they were, they would flounder in the melting snow in the woods.

When he heard the shot he began to run, instinctively, without thinking about it. Then he thought about Adam and he turned to look. Adam was running, too, but he was zigzagging as if he didn't know which way to run. Blood streamed down the side of his face from a deep furrow over his left ear. He had lost his cap.

Joel swerved and ran over to him. "Adam! Listen to me!"

Adam looked at him blankly. He tugged at Adam's sleeve and pointed to the creek. Adam nodded obediently and

107

set off in the right direction. If only there weren't two men on the ridge! It would take one man time to reload. But two men—the second man might be aiming at him now. He felt the fear prickles running up his spine. Even with a musket, you could hit a target as close as he and Adam were. And that had been a rifle, he'd swear.

The rifle cracked again, just as they reached the edge of the creek. The ball droned just overhead and a piece of bark flew off the trunk of a giant maple in their path. He pulled Adam after him onto the ice and beyond the shadow of the ridge. And then Adam grinned at him and sat down.

Now he knew what it was. If the ball had gone through Adam's skull, Adam would be dead by now. What must have happened was that the ball had just grazed Adam and knocked him silly. Some of the hunters up around Edmeston had bragged about how they could shoot at a squirrel that way and knock it out of a tree without even touching it. "Barking" was what they had called it. The ball stayed in the bark of the tree where it could be retrieved and used again.

There was one good thing about it, though. Adam had hung onto the loaded muskets. He took one now and pulled the hammer back to full cock and laid it down on the ice beside him. Then he loosened the carrying strap and let the three unloaded pieces fall behind him.

The next thing to do was to get a bandage on Adam's head. He reached under his hunting shirt until he felt the linen of his undershirt. He tore off a strip and made a pad of it. It probably wasn't too clean, but it would be better than nothing. He put the pad over the furrow above Adam's ear and took off his cap and jammed it on Adam's head so that it held the pad in place.

Adam looked troubled. His eyes questioned Joel and suddenly terror showed.

"It's all right, Adam," Joel said easily. "He just came close. You aren't hurt too bad."

Adam nodded. "What happened?"

"We've been shot at," he said slowly. "Somebody is following us. Do you understand?"

Sudden comprehension dawned in Adam's face. "I'm all right, Joel. I'm fine, now."

Joel grinned with relief. "All right, Adam. Keep low and do everything I do. All right?"

Adam nodded and cocked the musket in his hand. "Where do we go now?"

"We stay low so the bank of the creek will cover us. He's on the ridge east of the house and we've been moving north. He's probably going along the ridge to cut us off, so we're going to head south, because he won't expect us to move towards him."

Adam nodded. "Let's go," he said gamely.

When they had reached the southern end of the clearing, Joel held up his hand to halt Adam. He picked up a forked branch from the surface of the ice. "Give me your cap," he ordered Adam.

He carefully wedged the cap on the branch and held it over the edge of the bank, carefully turning it this way and that, to simulate a man looking around. Suddenly the cap jumped off the stick, and in the next moment he heard the crack of the rifle, ringing across the hollow bowl of the clearing. The sniper had guessed wrong, judging from the range. He had moved further north along the ridge, and now he was a good four hundred yards away. He could tell by the sound of the rifle.

"Well," he said to Adam. "He's still up there."

Adam picked up Joel's cap and put it back on, carefully arranging the pad under it. "He sure is," he said, trying to keep his voice steady. "What do we do about it?"

"Get up on the ridge ourselves, where we have a chance

109

to see him first. There's a rocky place up ahead where we can sit and wait him out. We'll climb the ridge just beyond the bend."

The sun was warm on the bare rock. They waited through the noontide, watching the ridge across the clearing and the place where the rocks were swallowed by the timber. They waited while the sun went past the meridian, and then Adam crawled closer to Joel.

"I'm getting cold," he said. "And my head started to bleed again when I moved it, a while back."

"All right," Joel said. "It's probably safe enough to move now. It's been three hours, at least."

"What's he doing, do you suppose?"

"Walking up the creek bed, I hope. Because if he isn't doing that, then he's going for help." He stood up and adjusted the strap of the unloaded muskets over his shoulder again.

"Come on," he said. "Let's make tracks."

ELEVEN

JOEL tried to put himself in the place of the man who had fired on them. It seemed likely that he was the same man who had placed the pouch and the muskets in the chimney. That meant that he would want to stop them from getting back to town with the muskets. Since he had failed to find them so far, he was probably waiting for them to start back. Sooner or later, they would have to come through the woods to the road, and he would probably try to intercept them there.

There was only one thing to do. Adam needed help soon, and that meant that they had to get back to the doctor. They would have to take a wide turn through the woods and approach the town from a different direction in order to avoid the man with the rifle.

Joel led the way down the ridge to the place where the trail led into the timber. Then he branched off to the south, following a little ravine that he knew would carry them around the flank of the mountain that lay between them and Goshen. The route would be about a mile longer, but it would be easier traveling for Adam.

Adam was only carrying one of the muskets now, while Joel carried the other loaded one in addition to the three which he had strapped together. Down in the ravine, the snow was still frozen, and for a while they made good time. He pushed on as fast as he could without being foolhardy. There was always a chance that the man with the rifle had seen them leaving the ridge and that he would be able to get ahead of them and lay an ambush.

111

But nothing happened. By the time the ravine petered out, the heat of the sun was gone and the snow on the exposed flanks had begun to freeze. He stopped and checked his bearings. One way or another, they had to be about two miles south of Goshen and about a mile west. That was perfect. If they cut across the timber tract directly ahead, they would come out on the south edge of the doctor's fields, and then they would have less than a mile to walk across the field. It was the way he had come with Sergeant Ford's patrol. He turned to look down the back trail.

A quarter of a mile behind him, there was a black spot in the snow. Adam!

He chided himself for having forgotten Adam in the confusion of trying to keep his bearings over an unfamiliar route and of worrying about the rifleman who had surprised them at the claim. He loosened the strap that held the three muskets on his shoulder and let them slide down to the ground. Then he put down his own musket and ran back along the trail.

Adam smiled faintly. "Sorry, Joel," he mumbled. "I was just resting for a while."

"Why, sure," he told Adam. "Let me give you a hand up. We're pretty nearly there."

Adam got to his feet, tottering slightly under the strain. Joel picked up the musket Adam had been carrying and checked the muzzle to make sure it wasn't jammed full of snow. Many a careless hunter had jammed his gun muzzle with snow or mud and then had the musket blow up in his face when he tried to fire it.

There was no doubt but that Adam had about reached the end of his tether. He took a few tentative steps and then smiled apologetically and sadly—and sat down. "Let's see how well you know your Latin verbs," he said conversationally.

"How about waiting until we get to some place where it's warm, Adam? Maybe we can get something to eat, too."

Adam shook his head. "Not hungry," he announced. "Not cold, either. Just fine."

Joel got one arm around Adam's waist and heaved him to his feet. "Put an arm over my shoulder," he ordered. "You can't stay out here. You'd freeze to death before I could get help for you."

Adam didn't answer, but he obeyed. Joel helped him along until they got back to the place where he had left the other muskets. Then he let Adam sit down again while he searched for a place to leave them. It was unlikely that anyone would come this way before he could return, but it was better to be safe than sorry. He walked off the trail until he found a fissure in the rock face of the mountain. He thrust the muskets in, the three unloaded ones and the loaded one he had carried. Then he stepped backwards two or three paces until he could no longer see them. Satisfied, he went back to Adam.

By the time he got Adam to the edge of the doctor's fields, the light was beginning to fade. In a way that was good, because if the man with the rifle had guessed that they had taken a different way back, he would have a harder time seeing them. On the other hand, Joel would have a harder time finding the muskets, if it got too dark. A lot depended upon what the sniper had done. Had he gone for help? Or had he worked his way along the bed of the creek searching for footprints? Had he found the place where they had hidden in the rocks and was he on their back trail now?

Stop it, Joel ordered himself. In another minute you'll see Joseph Brant's Indians in front of you and John Butler's Rangers behind you and the whole British Army spread out on the sides. Just work at getting Adam to the doctor's house. Never mind the man who shot at you. If you get Adam out of this safe, you'll be doing fine.

Adam seemed to perk up when they reached the level ground of the field. He moved along with small, jerky steps, but he moved without having to hold onto Joel's shoulder.

It was an improvement. Joel even thought about sending Adam on by himself while he went back for the muskets, until he looked at Adam's face. The boy's eyes were blank and staring. He could have walked right past the house without knowing it was there.

Grimly, he took Adam's arm and guided him in the right direction. Only another half mile to go.

Mrs. Tusten took one look at Adam and sent the children into the parlor. "Thank Heaven the baby's asleep," she said. "How did it happen?"

Joel told her.

"You were lucky. I knew no good could come of this going out in the woods all the time."

"When is the doctor coming back?"

"Heaven only knows. Susan?"

"Yes, Aunt Catherine?"

"Get out the pallet Joel used when he stayed here. Adam can lie on that next to the fire where it's warm. We'll put a clean bandage on his head, and that will have to do until the doctor gets back."

Joel followed Susan to the door of the hall. Behind him, Mrs. Tusten was already busy with hot water from the kettle and a clean rag.

Susan looked up at him. "I'm glad you didn't get hurt," she said. "I was frightened."

He grinned. "Nothing can happen to me," he bragged.

"It could so!"

And then he remembered. "Susan, I have something important I want you to keep for me. Will you do that?"

She nodded. "Of course, Joel. Anything at all."

He reached in his hunting pouch and drew out the leather pouch that he and Adam had found in the chimney. "Hide this and don't tell a soul about it until I come for it." He thought about it for a minute. "You can tell the doctor, but only tell him when you're alone with him. Don't tell him where anybody else can hear you."

She nodded again. "But what about you, Joel? Can't you tell him when he gets here?"

"When I get back. I've got to go get the rest of the muskets."

"Oh, no!"

"I've got to." He turned back into the kitchen where Mrs. Tusten was putting the finishing touches on Adam's bandage. He went over to Adam and unbuckled the straps of the ammunition pouches and put them in the corner away from the fireplace.

"How about taking off your things and getting comfortable?" Mrs. Tusten asked. "You must be cold."

"No, ma'am. I've got to go back and get the rest of the muskets before it gets too dark to find them. Tell the doctor I'm taking one ammunition pouch with me and leaving the other four behind."

"You sit right down and get warm!"

Joel grinned. "Sorry, ma'am. I'll be back to get warm shortly."

He nodded to her and got out the door before she could think of anything else to say.

Although the snow had begun to freeze before he and Adam had left the thicket, their tracks were plain as day on the level surface of the field. No one would have any trouble following them. Joel took a wide cast to the west in order to enter the woods at a different angle. If anyone were on the trail, he would not expect Joel to be returning. And if he had come as far as the edge of the thicket, he would not be able to shoot at this range. Not even with a rifle.

In the timber it was already dusk, although there was a good hour of daylight left out in the field. He wished he had a musket with him for protection, but it had seemed like a heavy load to carry when he had left the house. Four would be heavy enough.

He came on the rock sooner than he had expected to, and then he realized that the way through the woods had been shorter than cutting across the field. Besides, he had taken longer helping Adam to steer a straight course than it would have taken him alone.

He slid down the side of the rock and fumbled for the muskets in the gloom. When he had the three empty ones lashed to his shoulder and the loaded one cocked and in his hand, he felt a good deal happier. It was one thing to go up against an armed man when you had an even chance. It was quite another thing to go up against him empty-handed.

There was another thing that had bothered him back at the Tusten house. No one would go to all that trouble to keep two boys from walking off with five muskets. They simply weren't worth all the fuss. It had to be the pouch that the man was after. He was glad he had left it with Susan for safekeeping. If anything happened to him, at least the doctor would get it and find out what the man with the rifle had been so anxious to keep everyone from knowing.

He walked along the trail that he and Adam had used. It was hard to follow, now that it was getting dark, and it would be safe enough to cross the field, even if the man had followed the trail.

He had almost reached the edge of the timber when he saw a track parallel to the one he and Adam had made. He turned off the trail to examine it. Hoofprints! He was sure they hadn't been there earlier. The man had followed them on horseback, then. Probably he had followed them from town this morning. He had watched them go down to the claim and find the weapons and the pouch, and then he had fired on them as soon as they had left the shelter of the chimney. That explained the delay. He had had to leave his horse and go after them on foot, probably following the creek bed for a mile or two in each direction, not daring to wait for

116

them to start back for Goshen. And by the time the man had regained his horse and found the trail, he and Adam had been practically at the Tusten house.

His scalp prickled. Why hadn't the man caught him as he came back for the muskets? There was one way of finding out. He jogged tiredly along in the track of the horse.

The prints led as far as the field, and then they continued along the edge of the timber towards town. Joel pushed along until they merged with the frozen slush of the road that led south to the bend in the Delaware and Big Eddy.

He stopped to rest for a minute and thought about it. The man had followed his trail and Adam's as far as the field. That meant that it was still light enough to see tracks from horseback when he reached the field. Probably that had been shortly after he and Adam had come to the house. If the man had seen them without the muskets, he would have waited for someone to return for them. But if it had been light enough to see the track, it would have been light enough for the man himself to be seen. Apparently, he didn't want to be seen. That meant that he could be recognized. Joel grinned to himself. The day's events were starting to make a lot of sense.

By the time he worked his way back to the doctor's house it was dark, the kind of black dark that comes right after sunset and precedes a moonlit night. He got as far as the tree behind the house before he realized that there was a horse tethered to it. It wasn't the doctor's horse; when he felt of the saddlebags, they were unfamiliar. He was trying to make up his mind what to do about it; whether to stay outside until the visitor had gone, or whether to go right in and make the best of it. The horse solved the problem for him by whinnying.

Almost immediately the door opened a crack and the doctor called out, "Who's there?"

"Joel Benton," he answered as he walked up to the door.

Inside, Adam was sitting up at the table eating soup. "Hello, Joel!" he called.

Joel grinned at him. "Feeling pretty good, aren't you?"

From the far corner, Major Morgan stepped forward. His black cloak was mud-splashed, but his boots gleamed. "Adam Hanley tells us you boys had quite an adventure," he smiled. "Muskets and Tories and secret dispatches as well."

Joel kept his face straight with an effort. "Dispatches?"

The major prompted him. "Adam was telling us something about the pouch you found in the chimney."

"Oh, that." He deliberately stalled by putting down the musket he was carrying and lowering the other three from his shoulder. Out of the corner of his eye he watched the doctor and the major. The major's face was tense with suppressed eagerness. By contrast, the doctor was calm and unperturbed. But just then his eyes met Joel's and his head moved from side to side. He didn't want to discuss the pouch in front of the major.

Joel straightened. "Well, sir, we found a pouch in there, but we couldn't open it because it was locked. I had it fastened to the muskets when I started, but I must have dropped it down in the creek bed when I put them down to help Adam. Or maybe I dropped it climbing the ridge. Anyway it was gone by the time we got to the top."

"You put it in your pouch, Joel," Adam said reproachfully.

Joel shook his head. "That shot must have dazed you more than you thought. I only said I wanted to put it in my pouch. It didn't fit. Don't you remember?" He opened the flap of his pouch as proof.

Adam looked bewildered. "If you say so . . . I don't remember any of it too well."

The major smiled urbanely. "Well, it was quite an adventure, one way or another. I believe I'd better get going. I'd like to see Captain Brown this evening, and then I'd like to get some sleep. I was down near the Delaware today, checking the settlers to make sure that they knew what they were supposed to do. Your servant, Colonel." He smiled briefly at Adam and Joel. "Gentlemen, goodnight."

The door closed behind the major and a moment later his horse clattered off down the lane in the direction of the road. Joel went to the door and listened. The doctor watched Joel with a faint smile.

"He's headed west," Joel said.

The doctor nodded. "I thought so. Captain Brown lives east of here," he added casually.

"The man who followed us was on horseback. I couldn't tell much from the tracks, because you can't get a clear print in melting snow, so I couldn't prove anything."

The doctor nodded. "I just had a dispatch today from Colonel Hathorn. I had written him last week to inquire about Major Morgan's credentials. He sounded somewhat surprised that I could question them. He said the major was completely trustworthy. Does that answer the question you haven't asked?"

"No, sir. The major was entirely too curious about that pouch. He brought up the subject, and I'll bet a cookie he's riding back to the creek right now."

"I wouldn't be surprised," the doctor said drily. "Where's that ubiquitous pouch?"

"I gave it to Susan to hold until you were alone."

"Good work." He turned to the door. "Susan?"

A moment later Susan and Mrs. Tusten appeared.

"Is the major gone?" Mrs. Tusten asked. "Wouldn't he stay for sassafras tea?"

"I'm afraid our major may be a British agent, my dear. Susan, Joel tells me you're holding a pouch for him."

"Yes, Uncle Ben. I'll get it."

119

Susan had wiped the soot off the leather, and the pouch looked quite handsome. "A pity to cut it," Doctor Tusten said. "Can you pick a lock, Joel?"

"No, sir. We could take it in to Mr. Ford, though. If he can't pick the lock, he can cut it with a cold chisel."

"All right, then." He turned to Adam. "You'd better stay here for the night, Adam. If the major comes back, you may tell him that I've taken Joel in to see Captain Williamson, and that I plan to examine the claim tomorrow to see if I can find the pouch."

Adam nodded excitedly.

Susan came quickly to Joel's side. "Be careful," she murmured.

"I will. Don't worry."

"What are you going to do, Ben?" Mrs. Tusten asked.

Doctor Tusten smiled at his wife. "First of all, I'm going to find out what's in that pouch. If our major is what he's supposed to be, I'll tell him what I found. And if he isn't, maybe I'll tell him anyhow."

TWELVE

NATHAN FORD examined the lock. "It'll be easier to cut it than pick it," he said finally. "Do you care which it is, Doc?"

"Not in the least."

"All right, then. Here goes."

The cold chisel bit deep into the metal of the ring. Sparks glanced from the head of the chisel as the hammer rose and fell, and suddenly the lock fell apart.

Doctor Tusten opened the flap and turned the pouch upside down. Papers fell onto the workbench in a creamy wave. They were thumbprinted and wrinkled with handling. Something else lay on top of them. A cockade of white leather.

Joel looked at the doctor. "I knew I had seen him somewhere before," he said bitterly.

"There are many cockades," the doctor cautioned. "Let's have a look at the papers before we pass judgement."

There was a crude map of the region between Goshen and Minisink. Little squares represented isolated houses, which were identified by the names of their owners. A few of the squares had crosses marked in them.

"Probably Tory sympathizers," the doctor mused. "I always wondered which side Jed Perkins was really on."

Another paper proved to be a commission as captain in the King's Rangers, made out to one Arthur St. Clair. Butler's regiment, Joel thought. If only he had got to the doctor before the major had come, they might have set a trap for him!

The rest of the papers contained memoranda on the defenses of the individual settlements, estimates of crops and cattle, and an authorization for the bearer to recruit volunteers for service behind enemy lines.

"Well, that ties it up," Nathan Ford said with satisfaction. "I always knew there ought to be a good reason why I never liked the man."

"It doesn't tie anything up," the doctor said regretfully. "It simply means that there is a Tory working in this area. It doesn't tell us who he is. If there were a paper identifying Major Morgan mixed in with the rest of the papers, then we'd have good, substantial proof. The way it is, we don't even know how far we can trust the map. Certainly we can't go around arresting these people just because their names appear on a map."

"If we can't find Major Morgan in Captain St. Clair's pouch," Joel said reflectively, "maybe we can find Captain St. Clair in Major Morgan's room."

The doctor grinned. "Right! Nathan, get the nearest five men you can find and meet me at the tavern. We'll go over and have a look."

Doctor Tusten was disappointed. Somehow, there should have been concrete evidence linking the spy named Arthur St. Clair to someone in the town. The way it was, there was nothing. All things seemed to point towards Major Morgan, but they didn't link him to Arthur St. Clair.

He and Joel walked across the icy square to the tavern. The lights in the taproom shone cheerfully across the snow to meet them. He wondered how long it would take Nathan Ford to round up five men. Perhaps he should have taken Nate along to the tavern. On an evening like this, with a cold wind blowing out of the west, it would have been a cinch to find five men in the taproom.

But when they opened the door, the taproom was all but empty. Captain Brown was sitting in front of the fire with Captain Williamson, sharing a convivial bowl of punch. Joe

122

Martin, the innkeeper, was sitting on a stool behind the bar, rereading the Philadelphia newspaper that had come in two weeks ago. They greeted him and eyed Joel curiously, as if to ask what he was doing in a taproom. Then they went back to their punch, and the doctor crossed to where Joe Martin was sitting.

"Evening, Doc. Care for a dram?"

"Not this evening, Joe. I'm looking for Major Morgan. Is he in?"

Joe Martin shook his head. "Why, no. He was here about suppertime and he ate some stew and drank a tankard of ale, but then he left."

If Morgan had been here at suppertime, he had come out to the house afterwards. The doctor felt his original excitement returning. Morgan wouldn't have had time to clean out his room, to destroy any incriminating evidence.

"I'd like to go up there, Joe. This is militia business."

Joe's eyes widened, but he only nodded. "There ain't no key for the door," he said. "You can just walk right in, if you want to wait up there. Here's a candle to light your way."

The doctor leaned over the bar. "When Nate Ford comes by, send him upstairs, Joe."

"I sure will, Doc."

As he and Joel started for the stairs, Captain Williamson got up from his place at the fire and intercepted him. "Anything wrong, Doc?"

"I'm not sure." He paused a moment. "Suppose you and Captain Brown come upstairs with us for a moment. You can go back to your punch afterwards."

The four of them stumped up the creaking stairs to the top floor of the tavern and clumped down the hall to the small room at the end that Major Morgan occupied. He knocked on the door, just to make sure. There was no answer. He pushed the door open and the room came alive with the light of the candle he held. It was empty.

"What's this all about, Doc? I mean, Colonel?" Captain Brown looked bewildered.

"I have some reason to believe that Major Morgan is not what he seems to be," the doctor said reluctantly. "Joel Benton found a leather pouch containing Tory information out at his father's claim. He also found a cache of arms and ammunition. The major was supposed to be headed for your place when he left me earlier, but he turned off towards Minisink when he reached the road. He knew that the pouch had been found, but Joel here told him that he had dropped it near the claim. We think that he went back to look for it."

Captain Brown nodded. "It sounds like he might have a special reason for looking for that pouch, then."

"That's all I have to go on. There was nothing in the pouch tying it to the major. Nothing except his curiosity, that is."

"Well," Captain Williamson said drily. "Now that we're here, let's have ourselves a look."

As the doctor had feared, there were no papers of any importance on the tiny table in front of the window. There was a letter from Colonel Hathorn to the major, telling him that his report of the week before had been satisfactory, and another from the major to a Mr. Williams, thanking him for his entertainment while he had been a guest at his home in Albany.

"It ain't the sort of thing a spy would be writing, is it, Colonel?" Captain Brown asked.

The doctor had to admit that it was not.

"It's not likely he'd leave anything hanging around," Joel Benton insisted. "Not unless it was something he wouldn't know anybody could recognize."

Captain Williamson pulled aside a curtain on a string that screened the clothing pegs from the rest of the room. A suit of greasy buckskins hung from one peg. From another, a pair of soiled doeskin breeches dangled flauntingly. A powder horn and bullet pouch hung from a third.

"Not much here," Williamson said.

Joel Benton touched the doctor's arm. "That powder horn," he said, and his voice was tight and strained. "Does it have the initials C. B. cut on the side?"

Captain Williamson looked at him curiously. He took the horn off the peg and brought it over to the flickering light of the candle. The initials were plain to see.

"That was my Pa's," Joel said in a choked voice. "Where's his rifle?"

Williamson brushed the clothes aside and shook his head. "No rifle here, bub."

"How about the bed?" Captain Brown suggested. "It's the handiest place you could hide a rifle."

Joel pulled back the blankets on the bed to expose the mattress, a tick filled with straw. Then he tugged at the mattress and raised it off the cords that supported it on the bed frame. There was nothing under the blankets or under the tick.

"Look inside," the doctor suggested. "It seemed to be a little stiff, to my way of thinking."

The end of the mattress had been crudely sewed together with coarse thread. The doctor got out his clasp knife and cut the thread. Captain Brown reached for the end of the mattress, but the doctor stopped him. If there was a rifle to be found, it was Joel's right to find it.

Joel dug into the straw for a moment and then he looked up at the doctor. "It's here," he said in a choked voice. He tugged the rifle out of the straw.

It was a pretty piece, the doctor thought. The stock and forestock were of curly maple, the kind that was hard to find. It had the little bird's eyes in it, caused by projecting twigs when the tree was young. The wood had been sanded and polished until it was as slippery as glass. The butt was bound in brass and a tiny brass door in the stock covered a compartment for the patches. The barrel was octagonal in section, and a blued V-notch back sight and a knife-edge fore sight had been let into it.

"Great Jehosaphat!" Captain Williamson exclaimed.

"Can you identify it?" Captain Brown asked practically.

"It's a Golcher, and it has Pa's name cut in the forestock," Joel said. "Caleb Benton." He handed the rifle to Brown.

Captain Brown took a quick look and handed the rifle back to Joel. "It's his, all right. What do we do now, Colonel?"

Doctor Tusten pressed his lips together. Sometimes it was hard to remember just who he was. He had been happy being plain Doctor Tusten all day, concerned with the health of his people. But the time had come for him to be a soldier. A soldier acted promptly and efficiently.

"Go back downstairs to your punch," he said. "If Major Morgan comes in, let him get past you, and then take him from the rear. I'll wait up here with Joel and block him from this end. When Sergeant Ford comes in, send him up to me."

Captain Brown saluted awkwardly. "Come on, Ben," he said to Williamson. "Let's go ketch us a Tory."

Joel examined his father's rifle carefully. How many hands had it passed through since he had last seen it? The Tory had probably recognized its value and kept it with him all the time. He had been smart enough not to carry it with him, though. If he had been the man who had followed him and Adam, he had used another rifle today. Somehow Joel felt happier about that.

He slid the ramrod down the barrel to make sure the piece was empty, and then he carefully measured powder from the horn and poured it in. Then he took a paper spill from the table and crumpled it into a wad and inserted that. Last of all, he took a ball from the pouch and a greased patch from the patch box. He put the patch over the muzzle and rammed the ball on top of it with his thumb. Then he forced it down with the ramrod.

"All set?" the doctor asked.

"Priming." He opened the pan and poured in a small quantity of powder. Then he closed the pan and pulled the hammer back to half-cock. "All set."

126

Feet clumped noisily on the stairs and came down the hall. He pulled the hammer back to full-cock and pointed the muzzle at the door.

Doctor Tusten held up his hand in warning. "Wait," he whispered.

"Doc?" Nathan Ford said just outside the door.

Joel let out his breath and lowered the hammer to half-cock.

"Come in, Nate," the doctor said.

Nathan Ford stared at the room, and his eyes fixed upon the gleaming, deceptively slender rifle in Joel's hands. "Boy, where did that come from?"

"It was Pa's."

Nathan Ford looked at him. "You found it here?"

Joel nodded.

"That cinches it, then."

"It looks like it," the doctor agreed. "Nate, I want you to take however many men you've got and set up a guard on the roads coming into town. If he tries to come back, we'll have him."

"What if he doesn't come back?"

The doctor grinned. "We know where to find him. Out at Joel's father's claim."

They waited through the night in the small room on the second floor, waited until the pale fingers of dawn curled around the edges of the shutters and the last candle guttered out, and then the doctor nodded to Joel. "He's not coming back. We might as well go home."

Outside, the doctor mounted his mare and waved to Joel. "Don't worry; we'll get him. I'll send a patrol out right away."

A short time later, four riders trotted across the square on their way towards the claim, armed with a warrant for the major's arrest. Joel watched them from the window of Nathan Ford's shop.

"They'll get him, son," Mrs. Ford said just behind him. Her gray hair was neatly combed back, and her eyes were wise and kindly. In some mysterious way, without a word having been passed, he knew that she understood just what he was feeling.

"Nate says to get some sleep, if you can. He's going to sleep late, too; the poor man is all tuckered out. He was up half the night in the cold and the wind and all."

"Yes, ma'am. Only I don't feel too tired, right now."

She nodded. "I know how it is."

After a moment she left, and Joel went back to his pallet to lie down. He wasn't sleepy, but he wanted to think. As he pulled back the blanket, he looked up at the arms rack overhead. Nathan Ford's rifle and muskets rested on the pegs in order of descending value.

Joel paused a moment, and then he picked up the Golcher rifle that had belonged to his father from his pallet and put it in front of the musket on the second peg.

THIRTEEN

FOR the next week the town was buzzing with the news that Major Morgan was in reality the British spy, Captain Arthur St. Clair. Doctor Tusten, acting in the capacity of lieutenant colonel of militia, sent patrols around the town to investigate the persons whose names had been underlined on the map. Most of them proved to be perfectly loyal. Three of them, in fact, no longer lived at their former claims, but had moved to Minisink and Lacka-waxen after their homes had been burned the previous summer. Acting on a hunch, Doctor Tusten sent Sergeant Ford, Joel, and Adam out to investigate the three claims. In each chimney four or more muskets and their accouterments had been concealed.

"He was collecting arms to back a Tory uprising," the doctor guessed. "There would be no other reason to transport arms through the woods in winter. After all, Butler's men could carry their own muskets and so could the Indians."

They were sitting around the table in the kitchen of the Tusten home, Joel and Adam and the doctor's family and Susan. James and Thomas had just received their soldiers and the horse, which Joel had at last completed. He had whittled them out of pine in the evenings after his studying was done, and Nathan Ford had donated blue and yellow paint for their uniforms. Mrs. Ford had sewed crossbelts of white linen, and Joel had furnished each with a wooden, bayonetted musket. They looked quite warlike.

James took the musket away from his soldier. "I'll shoot him, if he comes back here," he promised.

Thomas nodded in solemn agreement, and Sarah held her doll against her in a protective gesture.

The doctor smiled and winked at Joel. "I think that the major will think twice about coming back to the Valley. The Minisink country is going to be too hot to hold him."

"I certainly hope so," Mrs. Tusten said tartly. "The idea! And I wanted to offer him tea the last time he was here."

Doctor Tusten threw back his head and laughed. "Something amusing happened today. I had a dispatch from Colonel Hathorn to the effect that the major was completely loyal and should be trusted with whatever information I could furnish him."

Adam stared at him. "Was this after you sent him the pouch, sir?"

"Oh, no. I had written to the colonel a week before we learned definitely that the major was a spy. Somehow I didn't trust the man. He wanted to know too much, and he never had anything to say except to tell us how lucky we were that we hadn't all been massacred last summer, and how we would surely all be killed next summer. I decided not to give him any more information until I had checked further."

"So the colonel hasn't found out yet?" Joel asked.

The doctor laughed again. "He has by now. In view of his statement of confidence, I should imagine he has a red face by this time. I don't expect to hear from him further, though. He's a proud man, is Colonel Hathorn."

"I heard today that they're collecting troops for General Sullivan's army, sir," Joel said.

"Where'd you hear that?"

"A runner came in from Albany. I guess maybe he was trying to drum up recruits."

"Well, I wish he'd drum them up somewhere else. The thing a lot of people don't realize is that in this war everybody's a soldier. Every man who lives here in the Delaware Valley is helping to defend the frontier as much as the troops in the Army are defending the seaboard."

130

Susan smiled across the table at Joel and he felt his blood stir. It was another thing they shared, their amusement when the doctor criticized the way the war was run. It wasn't that they disagreed with him, because they didn't. They respected him, too. But it was still funny to see him get worked up over the often incomprehensible antics of Congress and the Army. There was a certain amount of admiration in his and Susan's laughter, Joel knew. He had the feeling that if the doctor could only get down to Pennsylvania to talk to the Congress, a great deal of nonsense could be eliminated from the war. The doctor had a way of applying common sense to a problem that seemed to immediately reduce the problem to its proper perspective.

The only matter on which he and the doctor still failed to agree was his intention to hunt down the Tory spy who had been responsible for his father's death. The doctor had said that the man was no more to blame than anyone else on the enemy side.

"If you continue to hate this man and find him and kill him, then what?" the doctor asked.

"I don't know."

"I do. You'll decide that it was the fault of the Indians and the Tories who were with him. And supposing you find them and kill them, then what?"

"I don't know about that either," Joel insisted stubbornly.

"I can tell you. You'll get so used to killing people that there will be no other way of life for you. You'll never in this world make a good doctor or anything else."

"I don't know that that's so, sir," Joel said.

"Well, it doesn't have to be settled right away. Just keep an open mind and give the problem some thought. You'll come to the right conclusion, I'll be bound."

And there the matter rested. It was one thing to sit here with Susan and the doctor's family and watch the flames play with the shadows in the fireplace and think about being a doctor some day and marrying Susan and having a home of

131

their own. It was easy to see it as a probability, and it was easy to forget the man with the white cockade who had passed himself off as Major Morgan. But it was quite another thing when he was alone in the shop or walking the woods with Adam. Then he could remember all too clearly the other flames that had destroyed his home, and the howling Indians and the arrogant manner of the man who had stood by and watched them kill and burn an innocent man who had done nothing to them personally.

Those were the times when he wanted nothing more than to see the man with the white cockade outlined in the sights of the Golcher rifle.

He thought about it the next day, while he worked in the shop. Surely the doctor must be wrong about that. How could a man be brutalized by one act of revenge? Hadn't Hamlet in Shakespeare's play been practically ordered to revenge the death of his father?

The door opened and a hunter came in. He was dressed in deerskin leggings and a deerskin hunting shirt. He wore a heavy beard and his eyes were deep set in his skull, looking suspiciously out at the world.

"Where's Ford?" the hunter demanded.

"He stepped out for a minute," Joel told him. "Can I help you?"

The hunter laid his rifle on the bench. "I want the trigger-pull set lighter. This here drags on me."

Joel nodded. "All right. I can fix that for you."

The man sneered. "You think I'd trust a boy to handle this here rifle? You got another think coming."

A peculiar odor, musty and offensive, came from the man, and then Joel noticed the belt at his waist. It had a row of scalps fastened to it. Joel forced back a feeling of nausea.

"That's up to you," he said shortly. "It's your rifle. If

132

you want to wait for Mr. Ford, he'll be back shortly. You can sit down over there."

The man laughed. "Ain't you never seen Injun scalps, boy? That ain't all of them, but it's a starter. I'm going to get me a hundred of them or bust trying."

The door opened and the hunter turned quickly, one hand on the hunting knife at his belt.

Nathan Ford closed the door. "Hello, Tom," he said. "What brings you here?"

"How are you, Nate? I want the pull eased a smidgeon on my rifle. I want you to take care of it yourself."

Nathan Ford nodded. "Easy enough to do. You want to come back for it, or you want to wait?"

The hunter threw back his head and laughed. It was not the hearty, booming laugh of the doctor. It was more like the howl of a starving, rabid wolf. "I don't go no place without I have my rifle along. You get to it now, and I'll wait for it. Otherwise, I'll come back another time when you ain't too busy."

"I can do it now," Nathan Ford said pleasantly. Expertly he drew the charge and then he turned his attention to the lock. He unscrewed the lock plate and laid it on the work bench. Then he examined the oval-shaped screw that controlled the tension of the spring. Finally, he turned the screw a fraction of a turn, cocked the piece, and pulled the trigger.

"You try it, Tom," he said.

The hunter cocked the piece again and pulled the trigger. "Ain't enough," he said. "I want her so she'll go off when you look at her cross-eyed."

Mr. Ford nodded and drifted out the pin that held the sear in place. He carefully stroked the sear with a fine file and then he replaced it in the lock and recocked the piece. "Here you are," he said. "Try that."

The hunter touched the trigger with the ball of his index finger and the cock flew down against the frizzen with a resounding clack. "That's the one that did it," he said happily.

He stood by while Nathan Ford replaced the cover plate and screwed it into place, and then he made a funnel out of a strip of paper and poured the powder back down the muzzle and tamped the wad and the ball in place. "How much do I owe you?"

Mr. Ford shook his head pleasantly. "Not a cent, Tom. If you want to, you can drop off some meat next time you're in town."

"Much obliged." He jerked a thumb at Joel. "Take care of your helper, here, Nate. He don't look like he's dry behind the ears."

Joel checked the angry retort that sprang to mind until the hunter had gone out and closed the door. Then he turned to Nathan Ford. "My father wouldn't have let that man inside his house," he exclaimed.

"No?" Nathan Ford smiled. "That was your hero, Joel."

"My hero?"

"Why, sure. That was Tom Quick, the Indian-killer."

Joel shook his head in silent amazement. It was too much to take in all at once.

"There was nothing wrong with Tom until he saw his father killed by the Indians," Nathan Ford continued. "At first, all he was going to do was kill the ones involved. Only it didn't stop there. He kept on killing. Peaceful Indians, Christian Indians, women and children. It didn't make a particle of difference to Tom. Now he's got so he ain't quite human."

"That couldn't happen to me?"

"Maybe not," Mr. Ford said. "And then again, maybe it would. It's something no man can say for sure."

Of course it wouldn't happen to him, Joel thought two days later as he cleaned the Golcher in preparation for the muster. Tom Quick couldn't have been good before he launched his one-man war against the Indians. He must have been a cruel, vindictive man all along. But in the back of his mind he wasn't so sure. The doctor and Nathan Ford had both warned him that there was a difference between revenge and defense. The Bible was against it, for that matter. And when you came right down to it, what good would it do Pa? It wouldn't bring him back to life, that was one thing for sure.

Nathan Ford came into the shop. "You ready, Joel?"

He nodded and put his cleaning rag back in his pouch.

Out in the square, the early April sun shone on the gleaming arms of the Goshen Regiment. Joel took his place in the ranks of Captain Brown's company and listened to the commands of the sergeants and the captains of the other companies forming. Doctor Tusten rode his mare across to the vacant side and faced the three companies, and the inspection began.

"Private Benton," Sergeant Ford said to Captain Brown. "Let's see that rifle, Joel."

Captain Brown looked at the Golcher with a critical eye. "Any time you want to get rid of that rifle, son, you just let me know about it."

The man next to Joel snickered. "Ain't likely anybody'd want to get rid of a rifle like that."

Joel felt the proud blood rise to his face. It was something to have a rifle that any man in the company would have been proud to own. And then he felt a sudden pang. Maybe Tom Quick had been proud of his rifle in the same way. There was one thing for sure; he didn't want to turn out to be another Tom Quick.

The captain passed to the end of the line with Sergeant Ford, and then the doctor took the salutes of the three captains and ordered the regiment to stand easy.

"Colonel's going to say something," the man next to Joel whispered. "I can tell by the way he looks."

"How's that?"

"Any time he opens his coat up, he's going to make a speech."

The doctor was indeed going to make a speech.

"The formation of an army to destroy the Indian villages is official," he announced. "I have just received a dispatch from Colonel Hathorn to that effect."

The men were cheering, now; their voices resounded against the buildings that bordered the square. "Maybe that'll stop the red devils," Joel's neighbor said. "Maybe that'll show them."

"And maybe it'll only turn out that the warriors get away and the women and children get killed," Joel said.

The man looked at Joel with suspicion. "You sound mighty soft on Indians for a boy whose father was killed by them."

"I don't fight women," Joel retorted hotly.

The doctor was speaking again. "The cavalry force commanded by Count Pulaski and quartered at Minisink this winter has been withdrawn for service elsewhere. This means that the defense of our community will rest entirely in your hands. We cannot tell how much information the spy who called himself Major Morgan took back to the British, but we can be sure that he knows a great deal about us. Our plans are simple, and they need not be kept secret. We are going to defend our community against attack. We are going to go to the aid of any of our neighbors who are under attack. And we are going to pursue the raiders until we catch them and destroy them."

Wild cheering greeted the pronouncement. The doctor raised his hand for silence. "This is our strategy. If Captain St. Clair or Major Morgan or whoever he is wants to tell the British that we're going to fight, let him go ahead. This is going to be a hard summer for all of us, but at the end of it may lie the peace for which we all hope and pray."

The doctor looked around the square once, and then

136

he nodded to the three captains. "You may dismiss your companies, gentlemen," he said.

As the doctor rode away from the square, he felt pleased with himself. He had put the case squarely to the men and they had responded with all the fervor he could have wished. When the time came, they would fight, and they would fight well.

He was pleased about other things, as well. Nathan Ford had told him about Tom Quick's visit and about Joel's reaction to Quick. It was so easy to follow the wrong star when you were young! He was glad that Joel had had a chance to see Quick face-to-face and to compare his concept of the heroic defender of the border with the filthy, brutish actuality. Joel was an intelligent boy; he would make the right choice when the time came to do so.

But the doctor had less reason to be pleased within the next two days. One of the settlers whose name had been underlined on St. Clair's map was shot down on his own doorstep, apparently the victim of a super-patriot who preferred his imagination to the reasoned conclusions of the investigators who had questioned the man and found him to be loyal. It was one of the risks he had had to take in showing the map to the officers and sergeants of the regiment. Someone had talked to the wrong party, and here was the result. An innocent man had been murdered; his family had been left fatherless and embittered. Worst of all, an aura of mistrust hung over the community. Who would be next?

The next man to be punished was an old man by the name of Charles Higgins. He lived by himself in a cabin off in the hills. His wife had died years before, and he had never remarried. He was beaten somewhere along the Minisink road, but he managed to stagger up to the doctor's house before he collapsed.

While Joel held a candlestick over the kitchen table for light, the doctor undressed Higgins and washed his wounds with vinegar and water. His back was a mass of welts, apparently the result of having been beaten with a club. Other, lighter weals testified to the use of a horsewhip.

Doctor Tusten carefully felt of the thin, withered legs. No bones broken. That was something for which to be thankful. Old bones healed slowly, but given a month, Higgins would probably be all right again. At least physically. There would be deeper scars which would never entirely heal, scars caused by the realization that people he had known for years had chosen to believe him disloyal and who had then punished him without waiting to hear his defense, without bothering to learn the truth.

"All right," the doctor said to Joel. "Let's get him dressed. We'll put him to bed by the fire."

Joel nodded. "You handled him as tenderly as a baby, sir," he said.

"He was hurting," the doctor said gruffly. "He needs careful treatment. And a friend," he added in a low voice.

"Yes, sir."

The doctor looked up to find Joel regarding him with something like worship in his eyes, and he remembered the compassion in Joel's voice when he had spoken to Higgins.

He was satisfied. When the time came, Joel would make the right choice.

The first raid came towards the end of April. An exhausted runner staggered into town and all but collapsed on the street leading past Ford's shop. He was hysterical, and he babbled about a vast army of Tories and Indians led by the inevitable Rangers.

Doctor Tusten and Captain Williamson questioned him in the tavern, while Sergeant Ford and Joel looked on.

The man had been hiding along the river for a night and a day before he came to Goshen to spread the word. The small settlement of Lackawaxen, on the south bank of the

138

Delaware, had been raided and completely destroyed on the seventeenth of the month.

Worst of all, there was no hope of catching the raiders. They had attacked the settlement in the early morning, burned it by noon, and then disappeared into the woods without a trace. The man had no idea where they had gone. He had been too frightened to think of following them.

Doctor Tusten bit his lip thoughtfully. If he sent out a part of the regiment, he might be able to help some of the survivors, provided there were any. On the other hand, he might be dividing his force at the very moment when the enemy was ready to pounce upon the town.

"What about it, Doc?" Captain Williamson asked.

"Send a runner to Minisink to warn them the Indians are out, in case they haven't heard. Send another runner east with the dispatch I'll write for Colonel Hathorn. And get your company in marching order within the hour. You'll go down to the river and see if you can find any survivors."

"What about catching them?" Nathan Ford asked. "Weren't we going to chase them?"

"It's too late," the doctor said reluctantly. "If they were British regulars and we were Rogers' Rangers, we could do it. But we can't catch Butler's men. We've got to know about a raid pretty nearly as soon as it happens, and I don't know how we can do that."

"I do," Nathan Ford said. "Take some of the boys like Joel here, and send them out in pairs. They're good runners, and they aren't needed here every day of the week like the married men. Take Joel and Adam Hanley; they could range the country between here and Minisink today. Then another pair could take over tomorrow. And another pair the day after."

"Why pairs?" Captain Williamson asked.

"There's more chance of at least one getting back," Sergeant Ford said bluntly.

139

FOURTEEN

IF the relative mildness of the winter and the disappearance of snow by the end of March had not been enough to warn the settlers of an early beginning to the summer raids, the withdrawal of the cavalry detachment and the attack on Lackawaxen settled the matter. Sergeant Ford's suggestion was promptly acted upon by Doctor Tusten in an effort to provide an early warning system. The older boys and the unmarried young men of the town were sent out in pairs to patrol the country west to Minisink, and south to the bend of the Delaware River.

Two patrols went out each day, and the duty was rotated so that no one drew the assignment more than once in six days. When objections were raised by some of the nearby farmers who felt that their sons could be of more use nearer home, the doctor only smiled and said that it was a good way for a young man to learn something more about his country than he would learn in his own back yard.

The patrols were ordered to begin their reconnaissance at a point near the town, and to use separate routes going and coming. Each day they started before sunrise, waiting for daybreak at a point somewhere near the town, so that their departure would not be observed by any hostiles who might be lurking in the area. The patrols were rotated so that each of the men had an opportunity to explore a new area each week. It was part of the doctor's plan to make the boys familiar with the entire country in the direction from which danger would come.

But April passed, and May, without a sign of hostile

activity. The entire countryside lay warm and peaceful under the spring sunlight. In the fields, green shoots of wheat poked through the warm, brown earth, grew taller, whispered in the warm wind that promised summer.

"Maybe they won't come," Adam said hopefully.

Joel and he had stopped to rest on the crest of a ridge about three miles north of Joel's father's claim. It was a warm morning, and the moisture in the woods was steaming out in patches of mist, under the influence of the sun.

Joel wiped the barrel of his rifle with an oily rag from his hunting pouch. "I wouldn't bet on it," he said.

"Why haven't they come, then?"

"I don't know. Maybe because they're too busy up along the Mohawk. I have an idea that they're hoping we'll get careless and relax our vigilance."

"Maybe. I like my idea better, though."

"What's that?"

"That they've realized they can't lick us and they're not going to try any more."

Joel smiled. "That would be too good to be true. Besides, didn't they burn Lackawaxen? Their main reason for raiding is to keep the farmers from raising crops to feed the army. You can't burn green wheat, so there's not much point in coming down here until the wheat ripens. The only reason they struck Lackawaxen was to scare us."

"All I know is that some of the folks in town are saying it's a waste of money and time to keep us out in the woods. You know what they call us? Tusten's Rangers. And they laugh when they say it!"

Joel looked south along the flank of Shawangunk, where the sun touched the trees with vivid color. There was no sign of movement on the mountain, and yet several hundred men could have been hidden there. There was no way of knowing what lay in timber until you went in and found out. That was why you needed patrols.

"Let them laugh," he said finally. "They'll stop laughing when they find out the difference between being prepared for an attack and being caught by surprise."

"Maybe," Adam said. The chance remarks had stung his pride. "Where are we going today?"

"I thought we'd stay north of Minisink. I'd just as soon cross the mountain and stay north until we get past the settlement. Then we can cut south, maybe five miles or so below, and come back that way."

Adam looked unhappy. "That sounds like a lot of walking. Remember, we have to get back early tonight. Doctor Tusten wants us to come out to his place early and have supper there."

"I forgot about that," Joel confessed. "I wonder what he wants us out there so early for? It's not even the regular lesson night."

"I don't know," Adam smiled. "Maybe he just wants to save us walking all the way to town before we eat."

In the end, he had to compromise by staying close to Minisink and not pushing as far west as he had wished. It was still a change from the usual patrol, which stopped at Minisink itself, relying on whatever men Minisink had patrolling to furnish warning from the west.

They skirted the flat plains where the wheat and corn were growing to the west of the town, staying in the timber wherever they were able to. It was easy walking, and there was not much danger, because there were three or four claims inside the timber, near the top of the ridge. As long as there was no smoke and no sound of firing, you could be fairly sure that there were no hostiles out.

Once Joel stopped to look east towards Minisink. The sun was overhead, now, and the village shimmered in the noonday sun. It made a pretty picture; the corn ran down to the little river where the gristmill and the sawmill were in operation once more, and the wheat made even, light green squares where one man's field began and another man's ended. Corn shouldn't be planted that close to a town, though. If you planted corn that close to a town, you were practically inviting hostiles to come creeping out of the woods, using the corn for concealment until they could get close enough to storm the stockade. Even Pa hadn't wanted to plant corn that close to the house, except that he had had no choice, because there wasn't that much land. But there was plenty of land around here. Good, rich, rolling land.

Then they were past the village, and the flank of Shawangunk, the west flank this time, came closer, and finally he motioned to Adam and they began the climb. It was hot work, but when they reached the crest, some five miles south of where they had been in the morning, it was worth it. All the mist had burned away long since, and you could see the tall mountain over in Jersey, taller than Shawangunk even, and you could see the fold in the hills where Goshen lay. Some day, he thought. Some day the war will be over and we won't have to be afraid of anything. Some day I'm going to build a house and not be worried that it will be burned down.

Some day included Susan, too.

They reached the field behind the doctor's house about five o'clock. The sun had just gone behind the woods, and the light on the freshly plowed earth was soft and velvety. He and Adam dog-trotted along the furrows to the back door.

Susan opened the door for them. "Uncle Ben had to ride into town," she smiled. "He said to get washed up and we'd eat when he came back."

Joel took the bar of yellow soap and the basin she handed him and went back to the well to draw water. He gave Adam the soap and the basin while he carried the bucket, and then they went to the barn to wash.

It was pleasantly dark and shadowy in the barn. Mice squeaked in the hay in the loft as he poured water over Adam. Adam worked up a lather with the soap, and then he poured the rest of the bucket over him. While Adam was drying himself, Joel took off his buckskins and beat the dust off them. It wouldn't be long now before it got too hot to wear leather. He would have to see about getting some britches and a shirt. He could buy them over at Minisink, but he felt a little uneasy about spending the money. There wasn't much, and clothes cost a lot these days, what with the war.

Adam draped the towel over the side rail of the nearest stall and dressed. "I'll go get more water," he said.

By the time Adam got back, he had started washing with the water in the basin, so it was no time at all before he was finished. He combed his hair back and tied it in place with the bit of buckskin he used. If it got any longer, he would have to ask Mrs. Ford to cut it for him. It was the fashion to tie your hair back in a queue, but it would be hot in the woods in summer.

They walked up to the house companionably, not talking, pleasantly tired from the day's patrol. Susan opened the door for them again. The kitchen smelled as if someone had been doing a lot of cooking not too long ago. He wondered if Adam was as hungry as he was. From the smell of things, there was baked ham and squash and Indian corn. There had been some baking, too. Bread, of course. Maybe even cake!

"Adam, do you want to go in the parlor?" Susan asked. "Joel, can you take a look at the door? The latch sticks."

He went back to the door and examined the latch while Susan stood beside him watching. He worked it up and down a couple of times, but he could find nothing wrong with it. "Maybe it needs a little oil," he said finally. "If you've got some tallow handy, I could try that."

Obediently, Susan went over to the fireplace and got the pan of tallow kept there for basting meat. He rubbed the latch with a lump of tallow on his forefinger and worked it back and forth a few times. "That ought to do it," he said.

Susan was smiling at him as if he had done something wonderful. "Let's us go in the parlor, too," she said.

The parlor was dim, and at first he couldn't see them

standing in the far corner. He stopped and blinked, and then they all yelled, "Surprise, Joel! Happy Birthday!"

He stood there for a minute, feeling like some kind of fool, and then he grinned and said, "Thank you," and then they all crowded around him, the doctor and Mrs. Tusten and the children, Mr. and Mrs. Ford, and the Reverend and Mrs. Hanley.

"How did you know when my birthday was?" he asked finally.

"From the muster rolls," the doctor chuckled. "We thought that we ought to do something to celebrate the birthday of the boy who flushed a Tory spy for us, so we looked."

"It was certainly a happy day for us, Joel," the Reverend Hanley added. He reached in the tail pocket of his coat and drew out a small, black book. "A little memento of the occasion, Joel. The Holy Bible."

Joel swallowed. "I'm grateful to you, sir," he managed to mumble.

Mrs. Ford came over with her husband. "This is for you, Joel." She held out a pair of stout corduroy britches. "I made them out of a suit of Nate's he never wore." Abruptly she leaned up and kissed him. "Bless you, boy," she said.

Nathan Ford grinned at him. "If you was a little older, Joel, I'd be jealous. But the way it is—Happy Birthday!"

Mrs. Tusten was next with a pair of sturdy-looking shoes. "The doctor and I thought you'd be more comfortable this summer in shoes, at least while you aren't out in the woods." She smiled at him and then she, too, kissed him. "We're glad to have you near us, Joel. You're one of the family."

Susan had slipped away while the presents were being given, and now she reappeared in the doorway. "Is anyone hungry?" she called.

They went into the kitchen again. The table had been set with a white tablecloth and the good china and glassware that had belonged to the doctor's mother. A pitcher of cider

146

stood near the doctor's place, and a succulent ham squatted appetizingly on a platter near it.

As Joel hesitated in the doorway, the doctor touched his arm. "I have something for you too, Joel," he said. "You can't see it or touch it, but it's there. At the end of summer I'm going to take you in as my full-time assistant and keep you for a year. When the year is up, I'm sending you to Doctor Burnet in Newark. I studied under him myself. You see, he's an old man now, and he'll have more time to spend with you. I've arranged to have all your expenses taken care of."

Joel looked at him. "Sir, I don't know what to say. 'Thank you' isn't enough."

"Why, of course it is, boy," the doctor smiled. "The only thing I ask is that you try as hard as you can. If you try hard enough at anything, it doesn't matter what you are, you'll be happy." The doctor chuckled. "Besides, who knows? You might be an even closer member of the family some day."

Joel felt himself blushing and then he began to laugh along with the doctor.

"Ben!" Mrs. Tusten called. "Why don't you and Joel come in and sit down, instead of standing there telling secrets to each other?"

James and Thomas ran across the room and seized Joel by the hand. "Come on, Joel! We can't eat until you sit down!"

Sarah smiled shyly. "We're hungry."

Under cover of the general laughter, he and the doctor entered the room and took their places.

It was a lovely occasion. Everyone said so, and Joel felt it. It had been a way of letting him know that he belonged to the Tusten family and to the community. I'm not alone any more, he thought. There's always somebody who cares what happens, if you only look hard enough.

The Hanleys started home first. Adam was tired after his long hike and said so frankly, and the parson was equally frank in stating that he liked to be in bed by ten o'clock, no matter what. The Fords stayed a little longer, because Mr. Ford wanted to talk to the doctor about a pain he had in his left leg, but then they started back, too. Joel stayed longest of all, because he had volunteered to help Susan with the dishes.

When they were all washed and dried, Susan carried them over from the table and Joel put them in the big cupboard in the corner, because he could reach the shelves that she couldn't.

"You're going to make a good doctor, if you can fix people the way you dry dishes," she said.

"I'm going to try."

"It doesn't matter whether you're a doctor or not, Joel," she said gravely. "Whatever you do, you're going to be good at it. I know."

"That's mighty kind of you to say so."

She flushed. "Well, I mean it! I have a present for you, too. Wait a minute." She darted out the door and in a moment she came back with a neatly folded bundle. "This one's a white shirt for you to wear on Sundays or muster days. And this is a hunting shirt. I made it out of linen, like Uncle Ben's, and I dyed it with walnut dye."

He smiled happily. If a girl sewed two shirts for a boy, she must think quite a lot of him. "Thank you, Susan," he said gravely. "Every time I wear one or the other, I'll think of you."

"Unless you've got some more shirts, that's a lot of thinking," she teased.

"I guess it is."

For a moment it was almost quiet. He concentrated on the pop of a knot in the fire smouldering on the hearth and on the faint words of the doctor and Mrs. Tusten talking in the parlor.

"I saw something pretty today," he said.

"What was it?"

"Well, we were coming back in from below Minisink, and we climbed up to the top of Shawangunk. I could see the country for miles around. I could see the place where Goshen sits, in a little fold in the hills. You know?"

She nodded, with a far-away look in her eyes as if she were trying to see it, too, just the way he had seen it.

"Well, I was thinking how pretty it all looked, the trees and the mountains and the sky and all, and I thought about how it would be after the war. A man could build a house and he wouldn't have to worry about anybody coming to burn it down on him or anything."

"It sounds lovely, Joel," Susan said softly. "I wish I could see it."

"Maybe you can, some day. When it's safe, that is."

She looked at him, and then he knew he had to say the rest of it, too.

"I was thinking, it's going to be a long time before I can be a doctor; but by that time maybe the war will be over, and then I could build that house. I'd be mighty proud if you'd wait for me."

She nodded. "I'll wait for you, Joel."

He put his arms around her awkwardly, because he hadn't ever kissed a girl before, and then he bent down and kissed her and didn't think about it. It wasn't a thing you wanted to think about. It was either there or it wasn't, and that was all there was to it.

For a long, breathless moment she clung to him and then she broke away. Her face was flushed, but she was smiling. "I'll wait for you, dear Joel," she murmured, and then she was gone.

After a minute, he picked up his hunting pouch and his rifle and belt from the corner and went outside. It was fine and cool, and the stars were as bright as glass in the black sky. That probably meant that it would be hot again tomorrow.

He wondered if everything was all right with Susan. She probably would have said something if there wasn't, although you couldn't tell about girls. He knew that, because

149

Mr. Ford sometimes said that a man could never tell about women, and a girl was pretty near a woman, when you came right down to it.

And then he stopped worrying about it. He had a long way to go before he and Susan could think about getting married and building that house. But it was going to be a lot of fun, too, because now he had something to work for. He corrected himself. Now he had someone else to work for.

He was crossing the square to Ford's shop before he remembered that he had left his presents out at the Tusten house. Every single one of them!

FIFTEEN

JOEL managed to see Susan two or three times a week, although he and Sergeant Ford were kept busy in the shop. The last inspection had uncovered twenty muskets unfit for service, and most of the twenty were turned in for repairs—usually after their owners had attempted to repair them at home with notable lack of success. As Nathan Ford said, they probably wouldn't have bothered fixing them at all, if it hadn't been for the fines that had been assessed at muster day.

Generally speaking, the townspeople were inclined to minimize the importance of the Indian and Tory raid on Lackawaxen. The enemy had come and he had gone. That was all there was to it. The thing to do was to thank God that Goshen had been spared and to enjoy the blesssings of peace while they lasted.

The militia officers were hard put to keep the patrols sufficiently interested in their work. The men were restless, considering the daily reconnaissance a waste of time that might better be employed in getting ready for the harvest and tending stock. Colonel Hathorn himself came to inspect the regiment and made a statement to the effect that the enemy had probably learned of the punitive expedition that General Sullivan was going to lead against their villages any day, and that the Indians would be too busy defending themselves to consider any more raids this summer.

Doctor Tusten had the dubious pleasure of entertaining Colonel Hathorn as an overnight guest. He had to admit that he didn't think much of the colonel as a military leader.

The man was entirely too optimistic. There was no reason for believing that the Indians would protect their villages to the exclusion of all other activity. The Indians were smarter than that, even if Colonel Hathorn wasn't. Besides, it was bad business to tell the militia that their work was probably unnecessary. Too many of them believed that already.

When the colonel left the following day, Doctor Tusten breathed a sigh of relief. There were more important things to do than to worry about how many thousand troops General Washington had or didn't have. The important thing was that the Goshen Regiment had one hundred and fifty-two men, counting the officers and the sergeants. They weren't nameless, faceless numbers on a roster, either. They were friends and neighbors and relatives, and you couldn't lead them into any place that you couldn't lead them back out of. If you did, you'd have to live with it the rest of your life. He decided that he would let Colonel Hathorn help General Washington worry about his army: for his part, he would worry about the Goshen Regiment. Somebody had to.

Mrs. Tusten broached the subject of the regiment that night, when she poured his bedtime tea. "I wonder if Colonel Hathorn could be right? He seemed to make a lot of sense."

Across the table, Susan sipped at her tea quietly. She has something more at stake now, the doctor thought.

"He could be right, Catherine," the doctor said thoughtfully. "The thing is, you see, if I'm right in thinking that the Indians will come again this year, the preparation and planning we've done will be invaluable. If I'm wrong, then we'll only have wasted the time of approximately twenty-five men for five months. Since the men are rotated, and since they can be spared from their work, it isn't so terrible. On the other hand, if the colonel is right, all he's done is to save the time of those twenty-five men. If he's wrong, he could cost the lives of all of us."

"Uncle Ben?" Susan asked. "Why haven't the Indians come already if they're coming?"

"Crops, for one thing. They're waiting for the wheat

152

to be ripe enough to burn in the fields. We generally think of the Indians in terms of killing people, but the main reason the British are sending them down here is to run off our cattle and burn our crops. The British want to keep the army from getting supplies. They want to make us so afraid of them that we'll pull back into the forts and the blockhouses and forget all about farming. The minute the crops are ripe enough to burn, we're going to have trouble."

"I hope you're wrong, dear," Catherine said. "I've never hoped that before, but I hope it now."

"So do I," Susan said in a low voice. Suddenly the doctor realized that Susan and Joel had come to an understanding. They had acknowledged what he had known all along.

He smiled at Catherine. "And so do I, my dear."

"I don't know why you have to keep on worrying when the Indians have gone. It seems to me that you worry more now than you did in April, when they burned Lackawaxen."

"That's why," the doctor replied. "It's the thing you can't see that needs the worrying."

Joel awakened abruptly in the pre-dawn darkness. "It's time," Mr. Ford said from the doorway. "When you're ready, there's some mush for you in the kitchen."

"Yes, sir," he said sleepily. He knew that Nathan Ford would stand there patiently waiting until he got out of bed. The sergeant knew how easy it was to awaken and then to drift off into sleep again while you were thinking about getting up.

He dressed quickly and went into the kitchen. Mr. Ford had fanned the embers on the hearth under the pot of mush that had been simmering since the night before.

"Eat hearty, boy. You've got a long day ahead of you."

"Yes, sir."

Nathan Ford thought for a moment. "Last time you were on patrol you went north, didn't you?"

"That's right. We went up the Wallkill River and then

we cut through the timber for ten or twelve miles before we headed back."

"Today I want you to head west. Cross the ridge south of Minisink and head down the Neversink River. Cross to the west bank and when you get far enough so you can see the Delaware and the settlement down at Big Eddy, come back up the west side of the valley and cross over to the north of Minisink. Watch real close for Indian sign. I'm not too sure some of the patrols haven't been stopping short of where they were supposed to go."

Joel nodded and spooned up the last of his mush.

"If it gets too late, you can stay over in Minisink. Major Decker or Jonas can probably put you up."

"All right, sir."

Nathan Ford grinned and slapped him on the shoulder. "Good luck," he said.

Out in the shop Joel pulled on his linen hunting shirt, the one with the fringes along the sleeves that Susan had made for him. Over his right shoulder he hung the strap of his hunting pouch, and over his left shoulder he hung the strap of his bullet pouch and the thong of his powder horn. Last of all, he pushed the scabbard of his hunting knife to a comfortable position on his belt. Then he lifted down the Golcher rifle from its place on the rack and hurried outside to join Adam.

Adam was waiting for him in the square. He had been given one of the captured British muskets as his reward for finding the original caches, and he carried it proudly over his right shoulder.

"Where are we headed today?" he wanted to know.

"North of Minisink and west. First we go to Shawangunk and head south down the ridgeline. Then we cross the narrow end of the valley and head north, keeping to the west of Minisink. After that, we come back the easiest way we can, unless it's too late. Then we stay at Major Decker's or with Jonas."

154

Adam whistled softly. "That sounds like a lot of walking."

Joel grinned. "About thirty miles, give or take five. Want to start working on it?"

They walked easily across the square and headed down the road past the Tusten house. Everything was damp and pleasantly cold, and it was a little difficult to remember that July was already more than half gone, and that in another two hours it would be so hot that they would be raising a good sweat.

When they were three miles out from town, he halted Adam and they left the trail and sat down to wait for dawn. The pre-dawn halt was usually one of the most pleasant moments on the patrol. It gave you a chance to organize your thoughts and figure out what the day was going to be like. A rainy day in the woods could be miserable, and if it looked like rain, you had to reroute yourself so that you could avoid the swampy places. On the other hand, a hot day meant that you had to try to stay near water, if you could.

He leaned back against the bole of a tree and closed his eyes. This was going to be a good day. He had had a good night's sleep and a good hot breakfast. He could feel the mush in him now, warming and strengthening him. This was going to be the kind of a day when he could lick wildcats.

The only thing that bothered him was something the doctor had said two nights ago. The doctor had been talking about the regiment and he had said that he wished the Indians would do something so that he could tell where they were. The way it was, there might not be an Indian between here and Unadilla, and on the other hand, there might be a force of hostiles half-a-mile away. You couldn't tell.

Adam touched him on the arm. "Want to start?" he asked.

He opened his eyes. The mist was gray-white in the early dawn light. You could just about make out trees ten or twelve feet away. It was really too early to set out, in a way, because you couldn't see a whole lot. On the other hand, they had a lot of ground to cover today, and this was the least important part of it. The people who worked for Doctor Tusten would be coming through the woods in another hour or so, and they would see anything there was to see.

He nodded to Adam. They got to their feet and he took the lead, heading away from the road and towards the trail that he and Adam had followed last winter, the day they had gone to pick up the muskets.

By the time they reached the trail, the sun was well up, and they moved along quickly. There were no fresh tracks, and Joel wondered what route the last patrol had followed, the one that had gone to Minisink yesterday. Not this one, certainly. And then he put it out of his mind. When you were walking the woods, it was far safer to keep your eyes open and your mind on what you were doing now, than to worry about what other people hadn't done yesterday.

By the time Joel and Adam had reached the point on the ridge from which they could see the Delaware curve to the south, it was past noon; and it was late in the afternoon before they had worked their way across the valley and into the timber on the other side.

Just ahead of them was a low spot. You could tell that it was there because the ferns that loved water were starting to show up among the other small plants that formed the underbrush. There was a stream ahead, Joel remembered; it was the same one that led down from Minisink and furnished power for the gristmill. He motioned to Adam to come up with him.

"We can follow this up to Jonas' store, pretty near," he said. "We ought to cross at the ford here, or else go upstream where it's shallow."

"Cross here," Adam said. "I've had enough walking for one day."

"All right. Let's go."

They had almost reached the stream when he saw the

first sign of danger. On a small pine sapling just in front of him, two twigs had been broken. The needles were fresh and green, and the sap was still oozing from the broken part. Someone had been this way within the last hour. He touched Adam on the arm and pointed to the twigs. Adam looked at him questioningly, and then he nodded.

He found what he was looking for at the edge of the stream. The twigs had been broken by one man who had been off to the right of the main body. The main body was large, and it had followed the stream down the side of the mountain. Moccasin prints predominated, but there were the tracks of boots or shoes, as well. Did some of them belong to the man with the white cockade? Joel stooped over the tracks and watched the water in them, water that had welled in from the spongy ground. The level remained the same as he waited. That meant that whoever had made the tracks had passed some time before.

"Indians?" Adam whispered beside him.

He nodded. "They're going straight for Minisink, the way it looks. Let's cross over and see what we can see."

They crossed the stream and went a good quarter of a mile north of the stream before they turned east again and headed for the village. They were still in the timber when they heard the quick spatter of shots, faint in the distance. Then there was a flurry of yelping and shooting and howling all mixed together.

They came out of the timber at the north end of the valley, where it was only a couple of hundred yards across from the flank of Shawangunk. Below them lay Minisink, a scant half mile away.

The church bell was tolling now, and flames were rising from the two mills and several other buildings as well. The stockade door was open, and the village street was alive with Indians. As Joel watched, Jonas' store grew a plume of smoke, and then flame burst through the roof like a pale knife.

Adam shuddered, and then he lunged forward. Joel grabbed him by the belt.

"Let go of me!" Adam shouted.

"Keep quiet," Joel warned. "There's nothing you can do for them down there. You'll only get yourself killed or made prisoner. And then you'll be no good to anybody."

"They're killing people down there, Joel!"

He stared at Adam until the boy's eyes fell away. "It's over, Adam. They've done everything they can do, and there's nothing we can do to stop it. Look!"

Now they could make out some of the inhabitants of the village. They were huddled in a group in one angle of the stockade. Several men in green coats were standing in front of them, apparently preventing them from escaping. Several Indians approached the group, but the green-coated men turned them away.

"They're keeping the Indians off," Adam said. "What's the meaning of that?"

"I don't know. They're Butler's Rangers, from the uniform. Maybe Decker surrendered the place and the Rangers are living up to their word." He watched the black caps of the Rangers bobbing among the buildings. There were a lot of them, maybe twenty-five or so. Maybe one of them was Morgan. His hands tightened on his rifle at the thought.

The church bell stopped tolling and fell with a final clang as fire swept up the steeple, turned into a flue by the lower structure, which had been burning previously. Joel was galvanized into action.

"Can you get back to town by yourself?" he asked Adam.

"I guess so. What if they chase me?"

"You'll have to run for it. Come on."

The safest way would have been to cross the valley still further up, near the entrance, but that would have been an extra mile added to the day's journey, which was already considerable. Joel decided to take a chance. The ground was not entirely open; it was pasturage just here, and the grass

158

was fairly high. He bent low and walked rapidly across the ground, headed for a break in the timber on the flank of Shawangunk. Adam followed him, carefully copying everything he did.

At the edge of the timber, Joel stopped and looked back towards the burning village. There were no figures leaving it to pursue them. Apparently their traverse of the valley had not been noticed.

He set a fast pace for the climb. To Adam's protests he merely gave a curt, "Come on! Hurry!" By the time they reached the crest of Shawangunk, they were dripping with sweat and winded.

"I can't make it any further without resting," Adam panted.

"All right. There's a spring about fifty yards from here. Remember it from our first patrol?"

The spring bubbled from a cleft in the rock just below the crest. They drank sparingly at first. Joel put his head under the icy water until his scalp tingled.

"Don't lie down," he cautioned Adam. "You're bound to stiffen up if you do, and you've got a long ways to go yet."

Adam nodded. His wind was coming back, judging from his even breathing.

"I want you to head for home as fast as you can go. It's all downhill from here, or pretty nearly so. And you've got a four-mile uphill start on any of them who come over this way."

"Where are you going?"

"I want to cut along the ridge and warn the people lower down, near the Valley. Anybody who hasn't seen the smoke ought to be warned. There's some of them can't hear the bell, and if they aren't looking in the right direction, they won't see the smoke."

Adam nodded. "I'll tell the doctor about it. What if there are other Indians between here and town?"

Joel grinned for the first time that afternoon. "Just

knock 'em down as you go through. Tell the doctor and Sergeant Ford where I've gone, will you?"

"All right," Adam said. "Luck to you."

He held out his hand impulsively. "God bless, Adam. Take care of yourself."

He watched Adam heading down the eastern slope until he was lost in the timber, and then he set out towards the nearest clearing, three miles away. If the raiders were crossing Shawangunk to strike Goshen, the clearing would be in their path.

The claim on the ridge belonged to a man named McIvor, whom Joel knew slightly. He reached the edge of the clearing in time to see Mrs. McIvor emerge from the cabin, burdened under the load of a straw tick, and followed by five small McIvors carrying pots, pans, and a sack of meal.

"Ho, Mrs. McIvor!" Joel shouted.

She stopped and stared at him. "Hurry up!" she called. "You can come with us!"

He walked across the clearing towards them. Mr. McIvor emerged from the woods behind the cabin leading a plowhorse towards his waiting brood. He seemed surprised at the sight of Joel. "Where'd you come from, boy?" he asked.

Joel jerked his head in the direction of the Minisink Valley. "Down there," he said. "It looks like Brant's Indians and Butler's Rangers have taken the town. They've burned a lot of the buildings and they've got captives lined up. I came to tell you."

"Thanks," McIvor said. "Mighty nice of you, but I saw the smoke an hour ago. I figured it was time to move."

"It's time, all right. Where are you going?"

McIvor jerked his head towards the south. "John Slocum has a strong house and he only lives about five miles south of here. I made up with him that we could go there any time there was a raid."

160

"That's fine," Joel said. "It's further than that to Goshen."

"Want to come with us? We could always use an extra rifle."

"No, thanks. I've got to get back to Goshen. I'm in the militia. Tell the others down the line, will you?"

McIvor nodded. "I sure will. What's the militia going to do?"

"They'll be out," Joel promised. "Just hang on."

McIvor waved and grinned. "Don't lose your hair, son."

Joel nodded and trotted away from the clearing in the direction of Goshen.

SIXTEEN

WHEN he left the clearing,
Joel considered trying to climb one of the tall pines at the
crest to see if he could discover what was going on down in
Minisink. He stopped for a moment and looked back at the
pillar of smoke rising in the hot July air. Finally he decided
that it would not be worth while. All he would see would be
smoke; he probably would not be able to see what direction
the raiders were taking or how many prisoners they had. If
they were coming up the mountain in order to strike at Goshen, the best thing he could do would be to get there first.
If he and Adam were caught before they could carry the news
to Goshen, the raiders would have the crucial element of surprise.

He set off down the ridge at an angle, so that he would
pass by the clearing where his own home had been. It would
not be out of his way, and it might be valuable to discover
whether any of the local Tories had assembled there.

But when he reached the creek, the clearing lay dead
in the sun. He forded the shallow stream, holding his rifle
high in case he stepped in a hole, and then he walked along
the edge of the cornfield until he reached the horn of the
ridge that started behind the cabin and ran down to the
creek.

Once on the ridge, he looked down at the clearing.
The chimney had a green tracery of vines running up it, and
wild grass covered most of the plowed land and the clearing
alike. The marker on Pa's grave was barely discernable, even
though he and Adam had cleared away the grass and weeds

163

only two weeks ago. With the Tories and Indians on the loose, a lot of cabins were going to look like that. A lot of people were going to be buried in lonely graves.

He ran for a while, until he got off the ridge, and then he slowed down to an easy lope. He knew that there was a good chance that the party that had struck Minisink was not the only band of hostiles in the area; the enemy had been known to strike several places simultaneously before. But it was a chance he had to take. He had to assume that whatever lay before him was safe, and that whatever lay behind him was not. The important thing was to get to town with the information as soon as he could.

He reached the timber behind the doctor's house after dark, and he stopped to breathe himself for a few minutes before he covered the last mile. It would do no harm to wait and become accustomed to the dark. As he watched, lights appeared in the house; in the parlor and in the kitchen. He set off at a tired lope across the field.

At the back door he was stopped by a sentry who let him proceed after he had stated his name. He opened the door to the kitchen, where several men were seated around the table, drinking beer. He recognized them as the sergeants of the regiment.

Nathan Ford stood up and grinned. "Look what the cat drug in!" he exclaimed. "How are you, boy?"

"Pretty fine, Sergeant. I see the news got around."

Nathan Ford nodded. "Adam come in about an hour ago. He's in with the colonel and the rest of them now. The colonel said you was to go right in."

Joel knocked on the door and entered the parlor. For a moment he found it hard to believe that it was the same room as that in which he had received his birthday presents only a month ago.

The doctor was sitting in one of the straight chairs at

his desk. His blue and buff uniform coat was draped over the back of the chair. Captain Harper and Captain Brown were standing in front of the fireplace, and Captain Williamson was sitting in another chair, facing one in which Adam sat.

Adam's eyes twinkled mischievously. "What kept you?" he asked.

"Stopped to take a nap," Joel said. "I wanted you to get here first."

"Did you have any trouble getting through, Joel?" the doctor asked.

"No, sir."

"Adam has told us about the raid. He says there were about a hundred or a hundred and fifty of the enemy. Is that about the way you saw it?"

"Just about. It was hard to tell, with all the smoke and the running around, but I'd say about that. Maybe a quarter of them were Butler's men. The rest were Indians."

"That means Brant," Captain Brown said glumly. "I'd rather have Butler. He can keep the Indians from killing the survivors."

"I think Brant is an honorable man," the doctor said slowly. "I've heard people say that he's respected flags of truce and parleys. A lot of the atrocities laid to his account were perpetrated by Butler's men and by stray bands of Indians when Brant and Butler weren't around."

"I'll believe it when I see it," Captain Brown retorted.

The doctor winked at Joel. "What did you do when you left Adam?"

"I started down the ridge to warn the folks over towards the Delaware Valley. I got as far as the McIvor place, and I told Mr. McIvor about it. He and his family were all set to move to John Slocum's place. He said it was forted up."

The doctor nodded. "I heard he was doing that. He got burned out once by Indians. Now, he's got his house dug in four feet below ground level, and he roofed it with slate. Nobody can burn him out."

165

"Mr. McIvor said he would warn the other people down the ridge, so I came back in."

"Good work," the doctor approved. "You'd better get on out to the kitchen and see if Susan can find some mush for you. You can sleep here tonight, if that's all right with Sergeant Ford. We're going to move out early in the morning."

"Move out, sir?" Adam broke in.

"Yes, Adam," Doctor Tusten said gravely. "This time the raiders aren't going to get away unpunished. We're going to hunt them down and destroy them."

Adam looked at him and swallowed. "Can I go, too, sir?"

The doctor shook his head. "No, Adam. You're not a member of the militia yet. You boys who have had some training can be of value here in town. Someone has to stay behind to protect our homes."

Adam nodded, but his eyes were suspiciously bright. "I'll get on home, then," he said dejectedly. "Goodnight, gentlemen."

Joel went out in the kitchen with Adam. "I'm not going to say it's all right," he said. "I know how it hurts not to go. But if it's any good to you, I want you to know I'd rather have you trailing with me than anybody else I know."

"Thanks, Joel," Adam said. And then he was gone.

Susan brought Joel a plate of stew made with venison, greens, and Indian corn. They went outside and sat on the wide stone step, away from the men in the kitchen. It was cool, now that the sun had gone down.

"Uncle Ben has sent out runners to assemble the men," Susan said. "He wants everybody to meet here at five in the morning."

"That's a good idea," Joel said. "It's two miles nearer Minisink, and it'll save some time."

"What was it like?"

"Minisink? A lot of the buildings were on fire, and some of the folks were huddled up against the wall of the stockade.

I didn't see anybody getting killed. I'd guess that they were going to take the survivors off as captives."

"It seems so horrible," Susan murmured. "If only we could all live at peace with one another."

"I know," Joel agreed. "But it's a poor peace when one party isn't free. No matter what it costs, we've got to be free."

"The cost comes high," Susan said. "Are you going with them?"

"Yes."

His head nodded and he barely caught the plate before he dropped it from his lap. It had been a long, hard day. Tomorrow would be another one.

Susan took the plate from him. "Where are you sleeping?"

"I don't know. Here, somewhere."

"I could try to get them to move out of the kitchen," Susan said gently. "Then you could sleep on the pallet like you did when you first came here."

"No, let them talk. I'll go out to the barn."

"All right." She took the plate from him and bent over him for a brief moment as he sat on the step. "Dear Joel," she said, and her lips brushed his mouth. Then she was gone.

He got to his feet and staggered down the slope to the inviting bulk of the barn. Wearily, he climbed the short ladder to the hay loft and burrowed into the hay, using his pouch for a pillow.

He thought about Susan and her kiss, and then he tried to imagine how it would be when they came back tomorrow night, flushed with victory, and how proud she would be of him. But before he could picture it the way he wanted to, he was asleep.

He was awake at first light and he could see the early morning mists through the cracks between the boards. He lay

167

in the warm hay, remembering the day before, remembering the flames rising from the burning buildings as he and Adam watched the sack of Minisink, and remembering too the deeper color of the smoke later, when the raiders had fired the fields.

Yesterday he had watched the destruction of a town. He had heard shots fired. He had been close enough to smell the acrid odor of burning. But he had not been a participant. What would it be like to be in an actual battle? He knew what it felt like to be shot at; what would it feel like to shoot at someone else? He had never fired at a human being. Would it give him a blood-lust, as it had Tom Quick? Would there be glory, as Adam apparently thought?

Most important of all, perhaps, was the fear that seemed to lurk in the cold mists of the morning. Would he be tempted to run? It was one thing to run when there was no hope of winning a fight, and when no one else depended upon you. It was quite another thing to run when there were other people whose lives depended upon your not running.

He thought about it for a moment, and then he decided that it was something that you had better not think about too much. Fighting was probably like a lot of other things. When the time came, you would do what you had to do, and that was that.

He sat up in the hay and searched for his equipment.

Outside the mist was growing lighter. Men were coming up the road like ghosts, in twos and threes, in preparation for the march. In the yard, several of the militia were sleeping on the ground; they had apparently come during the night in order to be fresh for the march.

Joel went over to the well curb and drew a bucket of water. The windlass creaked and one of the sleepers sat up and swore at the disturbance. Joel smiled to himself and stripped off his shirt and washed. The water was fine and cold, and it smelled faintly of iron. It washed the sleep out of him, as he had known it would, and with it went the fatigue of the day before and the doubts he had felt in the barn.

He let himself dry for a moment in the sharp air, and

168

then he pulled on his linen hunting shirt and buckled on his belt.

The kitchen door opened and the doctor looked outside. He was in his shirt sleeves, but he was holding his uniform coat and his swordbelt in his left hand. He saw Joel and motioned him to come over.

"How about some breakfast?" he asked.

Joel smiled. "I could use some, sir." There was always something encouraging about the doctor's presence. It was as if you knew that he could take care of whatever might come up. It was a good feeling.

Inside the kitchen, Mrs. Tusten and Susan were busy with the breakfast preparations. Susan was stirring batter for hotcakes, while Mrs. Tusten was frying sausage in a pan. The rich, spicy odor of the frying sausage filled the room.

"It's better to march without shoes than to march on an empty stomach," the doctor proclaimed.

Joel grinned and Mrs. Tusten turned from the fireplace. "I've fixed you a package of cornmeal, Joel, and I found an empty bottle for water. Try not to break it. Bottles are scarce."

"Yes, ma'am. Thank you."

Susan smiled at him as she spooned batter onto the hot, greased pan Mrs. Tusten had used for the sausage. "Don't fill up on this," she warned. "There are eggs coming, too."

"Eating is one of the few unalloyed pleasures in this life, Joel," Doctor Tusten said. "Like the Bible says, 'Eat, drink, and be merry, for—.' "

Mrs. Tusten put down the platter of sausages with a crash. "Oh, Ben! How could you?"

Doctor Tusten looked properly abashed. "Now, Catherine. I didn't even think of the end of the quotation when I began. I wouldn't hurt you for the world, my dear. Don't you know that?"

"Yes, Ben," she whispered. "But it sounded so prophetic."

Joel finished the quotation to himself. "For that shall

169

abide with him of his labour the days of his life, which God giveth him under the sun." How many days? He knew the answer to that, too. No man knew how many days were given him under the sun. Perhaps the doctor was right. Enjoy what you have while you have it. Tomorrow might not come.

The doctor kept up a running fire of conversation throughout the meal, as if in this way he could dispel the gloomy cloud evoked by his heedless quotation. He joked about his patients, about the children, still fast asleep, and about his own ineptness as a soldier.

Once he caught Joel's eye and quoted again. " 'Whatsoever thy hand findeth to do, do it with thy might!' Sometimes it seems hard to discover just what work that is, doesn't it?"

"Yes, sir," Joel agreed. "I guess we just have to keep trying until we find out, don't we?"

"We do, indeed. The thing to do is to work hard at everything. You never know when it'll come in handy."

A knock on the door was followed by Captain Harper. "The men are all here, Colonel," he said. "Begging your pardon, but any time you're ready, we are."

Doctor Tusten nodded. "All right, Sam. I'll be out presently."

Susan came over to Joel with the bottle of water and a small sack of meal. "I put some sausage in, too," she said. "You might not get a chance to hunt."

"No," he said solemnly. "It was nice of you to think of it."

And suddenly he remembered that this was the morning on which the war was beginning for him. This was the morning on which his hands were to find different work to do, and tomorrow might never come.

Doctor Tusten cleared his throat. "I don't like goodbyes," he said. "But since we have to have them, let them be brief. And private," he added with a smile. He took Mrs. Tusten by the hand and walked with her into the parlor.

170

As Joel looked away from Mrs. Tusten's pale face, he saw that Susan was flushed. At times, the doctor's directness was disconcerting. Yet, it made things easier.

He took Susan in his arms and drew her against him. Her mouth was warm and soft and yielding, and then she pulled away from him breathlessly. "Oh, Joel!" she cried softly. "Come back safe!"

The door from the parlor opened and the doctor emerged. His eyes were suspiciously bright, and he blew his nose loudly. "There's an extra horn of rifle powder over the fireplace," he said. "Take it with you. Do you have enough balls molded for your rifle?"

"Yes, sir," Joel said. "I made up an extra hundred last week, and I oiled patches for them, too."

The doctor smiled at him. "Well, boy; we've said good-bye. Now it's time to act like soldiers."

Out in the yard, the men were sitting around in little groups, roughly corresponding to the company formations. The officers were wearing blue uniform coats that looked homemade. Only Captain Harper carried a sword, an old Navy cutlass in a battered brass scabbard that was suspended from his belt by a deerhide thong. Captain Brown had a pistol stuck in his belt, and he carried a light axe and a musket. Captain Williamson carried a twin-barreled rifle that Joel had seen before at the company drills. It was the only twin-barreled rifle he had ever seen.

Joel walked over to where Sergeant Ford was sitting. "Well, I'm here," he said.

Nathan Ford looked up and grinned. "It's a fine morning for a war," he said.

In truth it was a fine morning. The mist was already drifting away from the high spots; only the lowlands still held it fast, like balls of dirty cotton caught on thorns. Somehow, though, it wasn't the way Joel had imagined it would

171

be. There were no flags flying, except for the old rattlesnake flag with its "Don't Tread On Me" legend. There were no drums, and there were no fine uniforms. But when he looked at the faces of the men around him and saw the determination on them, he knew that this was indeed an army. A small army, perhaps; but an army.

Doctor Tusten had donned his coat and buckled on his sword, and he looked very much like a colonel. He walked down to the barn and disappeared for a few minutes. When he reappeared, he was leading his favorite black mare. He led the mare out to the lane, and then he called the officers to him.

The men sitting on the grass watched the officers standing in the lane. Their blue coats linked them in a group apart from the others.

After a moment the three captains returned to the men.

"All right," Captain Brown said to his company. "Let's come to attention, now."

With an air of unwillingness, the men stood up and formed ranks while Captain Brown and Sergeant Ford watched them.

Captain Brown turned to the sergeant. "Pick two men, Nate, and report to the colonel. He wants you to be the point scout."

Nathan Ford nodded as if he had expected the assignment all along. "Sturgis!" He looked down the ranks until he found Joel. "Benton! Come on with me."

They walked over to where the doctor sat his mare in the middle of the lane. "Here we are, Doc—I mean Colonel."

Doctor Tusten grinned. "Sometime I forget which one I am too, Nate. It's getting so I go to bed a doctor and wake up a soldier boy. Or maybe it's the other way around." He became serious. "I want you to take us to Minisink, Nate. Use the quickest route and set a good pace, but make sure we don't walk into an ambush. And make sure it isn't too fast for some of these farmers to keep up."

172

"Minisink?"

The doctor nodded. "We'll have to get over there and see if we can pick up the trail. If they took captives, they'll not be moving very fast. I'm hoping that they aren't going to expect pursuit, and that they're going to take their own sweet time about moving."

"Yes, sir," Nate Ford chuckled. "We'll do it the way Rogers did in fifty-eight."

The doctor looked down on the three of them, and his eyes caught Joel's and held them for a brief moment. "God bless you all," he said. "Now move out. I'll get the regiment started when you're a couple of hundred yards in the lead."

They walked down the road silently until Sergeant Ford held up his hand for a halt. "All right," he said. "This ought to be far enough. We're going to cut through the timber in about a mile. Sturgis, you stay about fifty yards on my right and keep your eyes open. Watch for my signals. Joel, you stay the same distance on my left. If either of you sees anything, raise a hand and stop. I want each of us to watch the other two every so often to catch signals. Is that clear?"

Joel nodded. "I've got it."

Sturgis wagged his head amiably.

"No talking in the woods. If you hear or see anything, stop in your tracks, and I'll come over to you."

Behind them, the doctor's voice came clearly through the bright air. "Regiment!"

The company officers sang out in unison: "Compan-ee!" A ghostly set of echoes reverberated from the walls of the house and the barn: "Ee, Ee, Ee."

Again the voice of the doctor. "Attention!"

For a moment there was silence, and then the doctor spoke again. "Captain Brown's company will take the lead. Captain Harper's company will take the second position and furnish flank guards right and left. Captain Williamson's company will take the rear and furnish a guard two hundred yards behind the main body. Once we start, I want no talking until we stop. We don't know what's in the woods, and we're not going to take chances."

Joel grinned at Sturgis. It wasn't funny, but he had to grin anyhow. It helped to relieve the tension.

"All right, boys," the doctor said in his clear faraway voice. "Let's get started."

Sergeant Ford smiled. "All right, you timber beasts. Fan out and get moving. He means us, too."

Joel waved at him and moved off into the underbrush along the road. As he entered the timber, he saw the trees before him brighten and take on color. The sun was up.

It was a fine morning to go to war.

SEVENTEEN

AS they moved through the timber, Joel became increasingly aware of the vulnerability of the column. Men in line made a large target, and a target which was almost impossible to conceal. On his right, Sergeant Ford moved steadily forward, hunched over to examine the ground over which he passed. Even at fifty yards, it was hard to see the sergeant at all times, and since he was constantly moving in a zig-zag pattern, it would have been hard to find any one moment at which he would have made a good target. That was the advantage of one man over a large party. He could go practically unnoticed, and even if he were discovered, he made a poor target.

But there was something else about the movement; it was the first time that anyone had done anything to attempt to catch the raiders. Heretofore, the settlers had run to the nearest stockade and "forted up," as the expression was, until the raiders had looted and burned to their hearts' content. Then they had returned to their homes, or to the ashes of their homes, and painstakingly repaired or rebuilt them. Not all the settlers, though; some had given up and gone to stay with relatives in the less vulnerable eastern part of the state.

By the time they reached the crest of Shawangunk, Joel was perspiring freely. It was a hot day, and no mistake. He was relieved when he saw that Sergeant Ford had stopped and was motioning him to come in. The doctor had ridden up and dismounted, and he was talking to Sergeant Ford in a low voice.

"I'm going to let the men stay here for half an hour,"

175

he said, as Joel came up. "We'll keep the points and flank guards out for security, but the rest of the men can have some breakfast, if they want it."

"Do you want us to keep on as scouts?" Sergeant Ford asked.

"If you're not tired," the doctor replied. "You're the best scouts I've got."

Nathan Ford looked at Sturgis and then at Joel. Sturgis grinned and nodded. "I feel fine, Colonel," he said.

"Same here," Joel said.

"Well, that does it," Doctor Tusten smiled. "Spread out again and rest a while, and then you can take us on into Minisink. I want the men to see what it looks like."

Nathan Ford nodded grimly. "It'll do them good. Some of them were complaining this morning about how we have to leave our homes to go chasing insurgents and how all the while the Indians may be waiting for us to do just that, so that they can attack the town while we're gone."

"I know," Doctor Tusten said reflectively. "I heard them, too. The point is, Nate, there are times when you have to take chances. If we don't hit the raiders when they come down here, we'll never hit them. And the more often they come down here and raid and go back unpunished, the worse the raids will get. You know that."

"I know it," Sergeant Ford grinned. "Try and convince some of these farmers of it, though. That's the hard part."

"We'll convince them, Nate. It'll take a little time and patience, that's all."

The downhill slope of the mountain was easier going. The footing was good, and the woods were deserted. When Joel looked down towards the McIvor place, there was no wisp of smoke, as there might have been, had it been burned. Log houses smouldered for a long time after they had burned. The big foundation logs could burn for a couple of days, especially if they were damp. It was a good indication that the raiders had not come this way.

There was a haze in the air towards Minisink, though.

176

He could see it clearly, and he pointed towards it when he caught sight of Sergeant Ford through the trees. The sergeant nodded to show that he had seen it, too. Nevertheless, it was a surprise when they came out of the timber and saw the grain fields that lay between the base of the mountain and the town.

The wheat had been put to the torch, and the fields were ankle deep in black ash. Even some of the pasture land had caught fire and burned in a wide arc northward to the end of the valley. The houses Joel remembered from his run to safety last November were gone, their places marked only by the smoke-blackened chimneys.

They moved across the burned stubble, spread wide apart now, and little clouds of ash followed at their heels. Joel was glad he was not in the column. The men at the end would be choking. Once he looked back and saw them slogging through the stubble in a waist-high cloud of dust and ash. They looked hot and dirty and tired.

Ahead, the outlines of the town were plain. The church was gone, of course, and there was evidence of burning among the houses on the outskirts, but a good many of the houses seemed to have escaped destruction.

When they were still a hundred yards from the nearest house, a man stepped out from behind it. He held a musket in his hands, and he called to them to stop. There was something familiar about him, despite his blackened shirt and his grimy face.

"Who are you?" he called.

"Goshen militia," Nathan Ford answered. "Is that you, Jonas?"

"It's me. Come on in and make yourself to home." He peered at Joel as he passed. "Howdy, bub. It ain't much of a town no more."

"It doesn't look like it. Adam and I saw it from the woods yesterday, and we went back to Goshen to rouse the militia."

Jonas nodded. "That's more than some of our people

did. They took off for the woods and never thought about letting Colonel Tusten know what was going on. They've been coming back all through the morning. Major Decker was wounded and he hid out in a cave."

"How'd you make out?"

"I saved the clothes on my back and a musket and some powder. The store's gone, and so are the sawmill and the gristmill and Decker's tavern. They even burned the privy back of the store. I heard the shooting and I took off. There were Indians in the stockade before I could get to it, so I cut through the fields two jumps ahead of the fire and made it to the woods. They couldn't see me because of the smoke, I guess."

In the center of the town, the damage was more apparent. The stockade had been pulled down and fires started under the logs. Most of them had gone out, but here and there some few still smouldered. A handful of survivors was watching them apathetically. Joel could understand how they felt. What was the sense in trying to save a few logs, when so much of greater value had already been lost?

It took some time before the regiment entered the town. The blazing heat of the day and the length of the march had combined to promote straggling; quite a few of the men were finding it difficult to keep up with the main body.

"It takes more than a musket to make a ranger out of a farmer," Sergeant Ford said succinctly.

Captain Brown walked over. He was carrying a misshapen black skullcap, of the type worn by Butler's men. "One of the devils lost this, I guess."

"Looks like," Sergeant Ford agreed. "What kind of guards do we have posted, Captain?"

"Williamson's company is spread out on three sides. Besides, we're not going to be here long. The colonel wants to move out in an hour."

"Which way are we headed?"

"Down towards the Neversink, the way it looks. Jonas

178

says they headed out that way. They were running a lot of cattle with them, so we ought to pick up the trail without too much trouble."

"How many captives?"

"I heard about twenty-five. It's hard telling, because some of the people haven't come in out of the woods, yet. Looks like they didn't kill too many. About thirty or so, Jonas said. They're laid out on the north side of town, and some of the men are digging the graves."

Sergeant Ford nodded. "About all there is to do, I guess. I'm going down to the crick and wash off some of this dirt. Want me to look for the trail then?"

Captain Brown nodded. "I guess so. You've still got the point, if you want it."

"I want it," Nathan Ford said tersely.

As they washed off the grime from their faces and hands, Joel refilled his water bottle. He had never carried one before, but he could see where it might come in handy. There had been plenty of time when he had been thirsty in the woods, even when there were no Indians out. It was a good thing to know that there weren't too many Indians out to-day. Jonas had estimated the enemy force at about sixty Indians and thirty Rangers. Surely the hundred and fifty men in the regiment would be more than a match for the enemy. He mentioned it to Sergeant Ford and Sturgis.

"I wouldn't bet on it," Sturgis said. He was a man of thirty. Before the war he had been a lumberjack in the woods along the Delaware, cutting the tall pines that were used for masts for the King's Navy.

"Why not?"

"Well, for one thing, there's no law that says that they were all here at Minisink. Brant might have split his force and only used part of it. Remember, he can call for up to a couple of thousand Indians any time he wants. And Butler's

179

got plenty more Rangers than the thirty Jonas counted."

Sergeant Ford nodded his agreement. "That's true enough. You take the prisoners, now. Brant is too smart to load himself down with twenty-five prisoners and cattle to boot. The only reason he'd have for doing it is if he expected to meet up with some more of his men in the next couple of days."

Joel had to agree with the logic of the other two. "But are you sure it was Brant?"

"You're wishing it wasn't," Sturgis grinned. "The only thing is, Jonas and half-a-dozen others said it was Brant. You couldn't mistake him. He's a real dandyprat, he is. Wears Indian clothes made out of British superfine cloth and a green coat like the Rangers, with a pair of silver epaulets on it that would knock your eyes out."

"Don't forget the hat," Nathan Ford said. "He wears a cocked hat with more gold lace on it than an admiral's got. You couldn't miss Brant on a dark night in a woodshed."

"Well, at least we've got more men than he had," Joel said. "If we can catch up with him before he joins up with any more, we'll have him outnumbered."

Sturgis nodded slowly. "That's one good thing. We'll need every advantage we can get."

"You can say that again," Sergeant Ford agreed. "I saw a lot of men falling out of ranks this morning because they couldn't keep up. And this here was an easy march, only a walk in the woods. Besides, some of these men have never seen an Indian before. They've run to the stockade and held a musket and waited, but they've never come face to face with a real, live Indian in the woods, where there's nothing to hide behind. And you can't forget Brant, even if Butler ain't here."

"That's right," Sturgis said. "Brant is an Indian and he knows everything there is to know about Indian fighting. He knows more about British fighting than most of the British do, too. He's had a white man's education, and he can talk the King's English just like a regular schoolmaster. If there's any way for him to turn the tables and give himself an advantage, he'll find it. You can bet on that."

"Well," Joel said. "I guess the thing to do is hope that everybody keeps up with the column and that we don't get sucked into a trap."

"That's right," Sergeant Ford said grimly. "I'm not worried about Doctor Tusten. He can handle things just fine, even against Brant. It depends on the men."

The trail of the destructives was easy enough to follow, as Captain Brown had predicted. In addition to the captives, they had run off thirty or forty head of cattle and several horses. It was difficult to be certain about the numbers, since much of the stock that was missing would doubtless be found wandering loose in the timber, but the tracks of the cattle and of the shod horses mingled with the moccasin tracks of the raiders and the boot or shoe prints of the Rangers and the captives proved that quite a number of animals had been appropriated by the raiders.

Curiously enough, there had been no attempt to disguise the tracks of the raiders. Either they had not expected pursuit, or else they had not cared whether or not they were being followed. By mid-afternoon it was apparent that they were headed on a westerly course, deviating ever so slightly to the south.

"They're going to hit the river and follow it," Sergeant Ford predicted. "It'll be easier going for them down in the bottomlands."

Joel nodded wearily. He was hot and thirsty, and he took advantage of the short halt to uncork his water bottle and take a long drink.

They were sitting in a small meadow, where there had been a clearing at one time. The remains of a clay-and-twig fireplace still poked above the grass stems in one corner of the area.

Doctor Tusten walked up to them, his boots crunching

the parched grass. "Left my horse behind," he explained. "No sense in making any more noise than we have to."

"Good idea," Nathan Ford approved.

"How old is the trail?"

"Yesterday's, still. They weren't in any hurry, but we have a lot of catching up to do. I figure they headed for the river. They have a lot of stock to water, for one thing. For another, it's easier going down there."

"There's one more thing," Doctor Tusten said. "They might take it in their heads to go for Lackawaxen again. They only got the houses in April. The crops were too green to burn. They might go back just to burn the crops."

Sturgis nodded his agreement. "That sounds like the kind of thing Brant might take it in his head to do. I don't think they've done it yet, though. We ought to be able to see smoke from here."

"It's pretty far. Fifteen to twenty miles, I'd guess," Nathan Ford stated.

"Where do you figure they stopped last night, Nate?" the doctor asked.

Sergeant Ford thought about it. "Well, if I was Brant and I had me a lot of cattle and prisoners and I wanted to hit Lackawaxen, I'd stop near water but I'd stay away from the river where they could see me. You know where Skinner's Mill is? On the little crick that runs down to the river?"

The doctor nodded. "Mill Brook. I know it."

"That's where I'd head for. There'd be less chance of my running into anybody I didn't want to run into, and I'd have plenty of water. And another thing; I'd only be about ten miles short of Lackawaxen. I could get up early in the morning and have the place burning by ten o'clock and have the rest of the day to escape in."

"Let's hope they did just that," the colonel said. "The men are pretty tired, and they won't be able to do much more. If we can make camp within striking distance of them tonight, that's about all we can hope for."

182

Sergeant Ford nodded. "There's one other thing, Doc. Don't forget that Brant may split his force and circle around to catch us from the rear. I'll send back word any time I see there are fewer tracks, but you'd better tell the rear guard to be careful."

"All right, Nate," the doctor said. "You can move out any time, now. I'll send word back for them to stay alert."

An hour later they came to a small stream that Sergeant Ford said was Grassy Brook. There was evidence of cooking having been done there, judging from the butchered remains of four cows and the black patches where cooking fires had been lighted.

"This is where they laid up last night," Sturgis said.

Joel prowled around the clearing in search of some clue that might indicate the presence of the man with the white cockade, although he knew that it was foolish to look. The man might be wearing moccasins, and then his tracks would be indistinguishable from those of the Indians. Besides, there was no reason for Morgan—or St. Clair—to be with every raiding party that went out.

The only thing Joel found was a doll made of a corncob, with a wooden head, and with a dress made of a scrap of calico. He thought about the child that had brought the doll this far, only to discard it. Had the Indians killed her? Had she managed to run away? What chance would a little girl have wandering around the woods, in danger from bears or wildcats, to say nothing of stray bands of Indians?

Sergeant Ford looked at the doll. "Poor tyke," he said. When you came right down to it, there wasn't a lot more to be said.

The regiment stopped for the night in a hollow, near Mill Brook. As Nathan Ford said, it was safe from surprise, as long as there were guards posted on the high ground, and it had water. You couldn't ask for anything better.

Doctor Tusten tasted the water and pronounced it good. "If there's one thing I won't have, it's bad water," he said. "How far ahead are they, Nate?"

"Can't tell. From the looks of things, they're taking their own sweet time about moving. I thought they might have stopped here, even though it's only five or six miles from their camp of last night."

"I wish I knew what they're up to."

"One way to find out. I'll go ahead and take a look." Nathan Ford motioned to Joel and Sturgis. "Come on, you timber-beasts. We'll go find us some Indians."

They followed the high ground through the long twilight, and when they came to a bend in the river, they saw the flicker of campfires and the shadows of men passing in front of the fires. In his imagination, Joel saw again the fires that had destroyed Minisink, the fire that had destroyed his house.

The land was flat below them, and there were few trees where the enemy camp lay. Beside the fires, a line of low bushes told of the presence of a small brook leading down to the river.

"Halfway Brook," Sergeant Ford muttered. "I might have known they'd stop here. They can move into the hills or follow the river or ford it about five miles up. It's the best place in miles."

Sturgis nodded. "I remember it from the old days. We used to get an extra ration of rum when we got here, because of the rapids a couple of miles downstream."

"No rum tonight," Ford said.

"Are we going in closer?" Joel asked.

"No sense to it," the sergeant answered. "We know where they are and we hope they don't know where we are. If we get too close and they find us, they'll be warned. Remember, they don't even know the militia's out."

"You better hope it's a surprise," Sturgis said. "Because if it isn't, we're going to have the fight of our lives."

When they regained the shelter of their own camp, the cooking fires had died down to a dull glow, and the men were sleeping in great black clots on the ground. Joel lay down in a clear spot apart from the rest and used his hunting bag as a pillow.

Above him the stars burned coldly in the black void of night. The grass was wet with dew, and he could feel the damp coming through his hunting shirt. It was cold, surprisingly so after the heat of the day.

Tomorrow would be the day of battle. The Indian camp could be no more than four or five miles distant, and they would be able to move in quickly, perhaps before the enemy was ready to move. He thought vaguely of the man with the white cockade. Was he sleeping in the other camp now? Would he be in the fight tomorrow?

And then something surprising happened. He found that he didn't really care about the man with the white cockade. If he were there or not didn't matter. What did matter was that one hundred and fifty odd men were banded together to make sure that the enemy would be punished so severely that he would never return, and that each man was fighting for what he held dear.

And then he thought about Susan.

EIGHTEEN

THE regiment was on the move before daybreak, and by the time the sky was light in the east, the men were approaching the flat land near the Indian camp.

On a signal from Sergeant Ford, Joel halted in his tracks. Ahead of him, the mist was knee-deep, and he knelt down to make a smaller target. He stared ahead into the mist until he could make out a darker sort of mist, dead ahead. The smudge from a cooking fire!

Sergeant Ford touched him lightly on the shoulder. "Let's go back and tell the colonel we're here," he said.

They waded back through the wet grass, their leggings soaked through and clinging to their skin. The regiment was halted, too, and the doctor had dismounted and was talking to a strange man in uniform. Joel looked at him for a long moment before he recognized the man as Colonel Hathorn.

"We're here, Doc," Sergeant Ford said without preamble. "What do we do about it?"

"Is this one of your officers, Colonel Tusten?" Colonel Hathorn asked with distaste.

"My best scout," the doctor answered, apparently oblivious to the scorn in Colonel Hathorn's voice. "Would you say there are any more of them, Nate?"

"I didn't go close this morning. I just saw the smudge of their fires and stopped." Nathan Ford thought for a moment. "I'd guess from the size of the camp and the tracks on the ground that there are close to a hundred and fifty of them. That's about fifty more than we figured on."

Colonel Hathorn grinned. "Good. The more there are, the more we'll get. Now here's how we'll do it. Obviously, they're headed for Minisink Ford. They want to get over to Lackawaxen and see if they can fire the crops over there. We'll go up the mountain and stick to the ridges. By marching quickly, we'll be able to get in front of them and beat them to the ford."

"We can't do that, Colonel," Sergeant Ford said patiently. "By the time we get up the mountain, they'll be gone and we'll have to go hunting for them again."

Colonel Hathorn stared at Nathan Ford for a moment, and then he turned back to the doctor. "Can you get your men moving immediately, Colonel Tusten?"

"I'd like to suggest that we attack now, Colonel. We can send one company out to the flank and attack with the other two companies in line. That way, we'll have them pinned, because they've got the river on one side and us on two. And if the Lackawaxen people hear the shooting, they can stop them on the fourth side. Either that, or else wait for the Warwick regiment to join us."

"Are you questioning the wisdom of my plan?" Colonel Hathorn asked icily.

"Yes, I am. You're not dealing with regulars, Colonel. You're dealing with militia who marched thirty miles yesterday. They're tired and they're footsore and they don't know about climbing mountains to get in front of the enemy. You may beat Brant to the ford, but if you do, you won't have more than a handful of men with you. The rest of them will be too tired to keep up."

Colonel Hathorn smiled through tight lips. "May I remind you that I outrank you, sir?"

"You may. May I remind you, sir, that as second-in-command it is my duty to warn you of unwise decisions? If you want to go climb mountains, I suggest that you wait until we get reinforcements. Maybe then you'll have something to fight with when you get there."

"Thank you for your suggestion, sir. I consider it of no value. Have the regiment follow my scouts. Captain Tyler and his men will take the lead."

Doctor Tusten flushed and then he turned to Sergeant Ford. "You'd better go back to your company, Nate. You've done well. Thank you."

"All right, Doc."

They watched the new scouts come to the front of the column as the sun came over the trees. There were ten or twelve of them, and they looked fresh and eager.

Sturgis spat on the ground in front of him. "I know that gang. They're from the Jersey militia. If that's all the men Hathorn brought with him, we're not going to get a lot of help out of him." He paused for a moment. "As a matter of fact, Nate, it would have been better all ways running if Hathorn had just stayed in bed and forgot to get up this morning."

"Amen to that," Sergeant Ford said.

The pace was fast. As the sun rose higher, Joel felt the heat on his back, drying his damp clothing, and then he began to perspire and his shirt became wet again. He kept his head down and his weight forward to maintain his balance on the climb. It was hard going, and no mistake. He wondered how the New Jersey scouts could set a pace this fast and still see where they were going.

Beside him, Sturgis slogged along, his face a picture of disgust. "Dang fools," he muttered. "The only good thing is that they're headed in the wrong direction to run into Indians. They sure won't see them at the rate they're going."

Joel swung himself around a boulder and scrambled to the top of a knife-edged ridge. Far below he could see the silver shallows of the Delaware coiling its way through the valley. A smudge of gray-white smoke betrayed the location of the Lackawaxen settlement on the far side of the river. He

189

turned his head to look behind him. There were only five men in sight. He turned to Sturgis. "Where's the rest of them?"

"Couldn't keep up, more'n likely," Sturgis said. "Harper and his company are down the slope, but it don't look like too many of them are there, either. And Williamson is supposed to be in back of us. He's a long way back, if he is."

Something moved down near the ford and Sturgis touched Joel's arm. "Look there!"

An Indian mounted on a horse was riding in the shallow water of the ford. It was odd to see the Indian without being seen. And then Joel realized that they were on top of the ridge, outlined against the sky. Unless a miracle happened, the Indian was bound to see them and give the alarm.

A shot cracked from the timber lower down, and the Indian fell forward on the horse's neck. He hung there for a moment, and then he slid off into the shallow water. The horse shook its head and trotted clumsily through the shallows to the far shore.

Sturgis swore. "That's done it. Now they know where we are. They probably know all about us anyway."

Another shot rang out in the woods just ahead. For a moment there was silence, and then there were five or six shots in quick succession. A wisp of dirty gray smoke rose over the trees, and then someone called out sharply: "Let's get out of here!"

Several more shots followed, and then there was a flurry of shots from the rear, perhaps a quarter of a mile away. Joel faced downhill to see what had happened to Williamson's company.

The men further down the hill were not firing. They were running up the hill, now, headed for the ridge upon which Joel and Sturgis and Sergeant Ford were standing. A few men behind them were closing up; they were men from Brown's company, and they looked scared. The firing from the rear had probably lent them an energy they hadn't had before. Colonel Hathorn suddenly appeared, red-faced with anger.

190

"Come on, men!" he shouted. "Close up and follow me."

Obediently, the men turned towards him as the firing in the front and rear grew heavier. Ford spat in disgust. "The idiot has gone and got himself caught in a trap. They're in front of him and in back of him and probably on the side, too."

Joel felt himself swept along by a tide of men from the company which had been nearer the river. Instinctively, they were coming uphill to gain the advantage of the high ground.

As Colonel Hathorn rode on down the line, Doctor Tusten appeared. His face was set and hard in the hot sun. "All right, boys," he said grimly. "There's a hill up yonder. Get on it and take whatever cover you can. It's a poor row to hoe, but we'll have to make the best of it."

Obediently, the men surged over the ridge and down the other side and climbed the precipitous hill.

The hill had a somewhat concave top. The ground in the bowl had been cleared at one time or another, either by settlers or by fire. Now it was overgrown with wild hay and studded with rocks and boulders. On the south side, just at the edge, there was a small pond. It apparently collected the rainfall from the bowl-shaped hilltop.

Already the thud of musketry was coming closer, and dirty smoke began to filter through the trees. Joel felt his chest grow tight, and he had to force himself to breathe deeply. If you were scared, you couldn't shoot straight and you couldn't think straight. This was going to be a day when both would be needed.

He went over to the edge of the hill near the pond and looked around for a rock to hide behind. A rifle cracked sharply, in contrast to the hollow thuds of the muskets, and a moment later he heard the whiz of the ball overhead.

"Get down, Joel!" Sergeant Ford yelled. "You could get hurt around here!"

He started to laugh, and all at once he felt better. He

191

nodded at Sergeant Ford and got down alongside his rock and trained his rifle past the edge.

So far there was nothing to shoot at. A few men broke through the trees, but they were obviously militia. They were running heavily, plodding their way up the steep hill. As he watched, one of them fell forward on his face as if he had tripped on a rock. Joel watched him, expecting him to get up again, but the man made no effort to do so.

"Don't shoot until you see something to shoot at," the sergeant counseled. "There's going to be a lot of our men coming up here before the Indians come."

A big, heavy-set man lumbered up the hill, stumbled over the edge, and then turned around to face in the direction from which he had come. Joel recognized him as Captain Cuddeback. He was a farmer outside of Minisink, and people said that he could raise his arms with a fifty-pound weight tied to each finger. He looked as if he were capable of it.

"What's going on down there?" Sergeant Ford asked.

Captain Cuddeback wiped his face with a beefy hand. "Colonel Hathorn ordered a bayonet charge with three companies in line. Half of the men don't have bayonets, and there weren't three companies in line, so it wasn't much of a charge. He had Colonel Tusten over here on the right and Colonel Wisner on the left. Wisner and a couple of his people showed up right before the Indians spotted us."

"That must've been a sight to see," Sergeant Ford grinned.

"It was one I wish I hadn't seen. Hathorn ordered the men in line to open fire at three hundred yards. Of course the ones with muskets couldn't hit anything at that range, and when they got all done shooting and got close enough, the Indians opened up. After that, there wasn't much of a line."

"I bet. We got in on the tail end of it. The colonel was hollering for everybody to come up here. Hathorn, that is."

"I know it. I don't know what he thought he was going to find up here. It's too far from the ford for the people over at Lackawaxen to hear the shooting and come help. And it makes it easy for the Indians to surround us. Maybe that's why we never made it to colonel, Nate. We had too many brains."

"You're right, Abe," Sergeant Ford chuckled.

The last of the militia made it to the top of the hill and scattered out looking for stones. Four or five men lay on the slope below the rock Joel had picked. They looked like limp rags flung down haphazardly. A few random shots came from down the hill, and one splattered against a rock next to Joel. He ducked involuntarily, and then he forced himself to look back down the hill at the all-but-impenetrable timber at the foot. Nothing moved, and suddenly the firing stopped. And then it was quiet.

Joel turned around to see what was happening behind him. Doctor Tusten had come to the edge of the pond and he was winding a handkerchief around his left hand. He saw Joel and smiled and waved his good hand at him. Behind the doctor some of the militia had taken positions facing in the other direction. Apparently there was no way of telling just where the attack would come. More men were struggling with boulders in the center of the area, pushing them together to form a sort of breastwork across the open field.

Joel counted heads quickly. There were only about eighty or ninety men here. There should have been close to the original hundred and fifty, in addition to those who had come up with Colonel Hathorn and with Colonel Wisner. What had happened to the others? He turned to the brawny captain beside him.

Cuddeback grinned humorlessly. "Some of them probably couldn't keep up with Tyler's scouts," he guessed. "Maybe they'll come up later, if they can get through. And some of them got killed on the way through the woods. That bayonet charge didn't do us any good."

193

"What can we do?"

Cuddeback stared at him. "There ain't a thing to do but set here and wait for them to make the first move. There's one good thing about it; nobody's going to have to worry about running away."

"Why not?"

Nathan Ford laughed from his position. "Because there's no place to run to," he said.

As the sun rose higher, Joel felt his shirt drying with a prickly feeling on his back. There was still no firing from the woods, and he rolled over behind his rock and worked his handaxe loose from his belt. He began to chop out the top layer of sod from the place where he had been, and then with the axe and his hands he scooped out a shallow pit. He trimmed the edges neatly and stacked the sods at the front to form a sort of parapet. It might not help much, but it was better than doing nothing. It kept him from thinking about what the enemy was doing down there in the woods.

"Benton?"

Joel turned to see Sturgis crouched behind him. "Glad to see you made it."

"Likewise," Sturgis grinned. "The doctor said to come give him a hand. He's over near that rock ledge on the west side of the field. I'll hold your place for you."

Joel nodded, and then he slid out of the pit and crawled away from the edge of the hill until he judged it was safe to get to his feet. He ran bent over until he got to the safety of the ledge. He felt foolish, because nobody shot at him.

The rock ledge was perhaps eight feet high and sixty feet long, and it ran across the west edge of the clearing. Several men had taken position on top of the ledge and were busily scooping out rifle pits in the turf that covered it. Under a projection Doctor Tusten was clearing away rubble that had fallen from the overhang, working with his good hand. Joel leaned his rifle against the rock and went over to help him.

"Glad to see you," the doctor smiled. "I'd like you to help me clear an area here, so that I can tend to casualties."

"How about your hand?"

"Never mind that," Doctor Tusten said. "I can do just fine."

Joel shook his head stubbornly. "Let me see it, sir."

The doctor held out his left hand, and Joel unbound the handkerchief. The palm of the doctor's hand had been torn diagonally across by a musket ball. "Nothing's broken," he said hastily. "It'll be fine."

Joel unsheathed his knife and cut a square patch out of the tail of his hunting shirt. He folded it into a pad and pressed it over the wound. Then he tied it in place with the doctor's handkerchief. "That ought to be a little better," he said.

The doctor smiled. "That's a good job, Joel. I wish I could keep you here as my assistant, but I'm afraid every rifle will be needed on the line."

Two men came over dragging a third between them. "Can you fix him up, Doc?" one of them asked.

"Lay him down here, boys," the doctor directed. "We'll have a look."

The doctor had prudently included his bag of instruments in his saddlebag, Joel noted. The saddlebag was lying on the ground nearby, and the instrument case was beside it. Joel wondered idly where the doctor's black mare was, and then the doctor called to him to bring over the instrument case.

The wounded man's forearm had been shattered by a musket ball. Splinters of bone protruded from the raw wound. Doctor Tusten held the man's arm steady with his wounded hand and probed the wound with the point of a lancet.

"Not much we can do about this," he said. "That arm is going to have to come off, but I can't do it here. The only thing to do is splint it for the time being. Get me a stick, will you, Joel?"

195

Joel went over to a nearby hemlock and trimmed off a low branch. "It's a funny thing," he said, as he brought back the limb. "You started out yesterday morning as a colonel of militia, and now you're back being a doctor."

Doctor Tusten looked up and smiled. "There's always work for willing hands. The Almighty in His wisdom generally provides a way for us. The only thing we have to do is look for it." He thought for a moment. "That's something to remember, Joel. Maybe you'll be a doctor someday, maybe you won't. That isn't too important. The thing that is important is that you do whatever there is to do as long as you're able to do it."

"How about now, Doctor? Aren't you needed as an officer?"

Doctor Tusten chuckled. "We've got Major Meeker, Colonel Hathorn, Lieutenant Colonel Wisner, and four captains. For ninety men or so, that ought to be enough officers. There's only one doctor here, though. I'd like to trade a couple of the officers for another surgeon."

Joel thought about what the doctor had said about work. It was logical enough. He himself had been able to help because he had learned about gunshot wounds and because he knew how to track game through the woods, and because he was able to repair a musket lock. Seemingly, no one of these factors related to the others, but each had served its purpose when the time came for it to do so.

"Speaking of work," the doctor said, "you'd better get back to the line in case they need you over there."

As he turned to go, the doctor took his arm. "Look!"

At the edge of the hill, the trees had been cleared for a long stretch down the slope, perhaps by the lumbermen before the war. Now a horseman rode out of the timber to the front of the position and stopped about a hundred yards from the line of skirmishers. He waved a white cloth in front of him.

The man wore a green tunic and a black cocked hat

covered with gold lace. His doeskin breeches were dazzling in the sun.

"By all that's holy," the doctor muttered. "It's Brant himself!"

The man's voice carried well. His words were clear and distinct, the words of a man who has learned a language other than his native tongue, and who is determined to speak it well.

"I cannot promise that I will be able to restrain my men once we attack. I give you my word that if you lay down your arms and promise to go back to your homes I will spare your lives." He paused for breath. "But you must do this now, before the fighting begins."

Joel looked at the doctor. "Does he mean that?"

"I don't know. I think he does."

"You are surrounded on four sides," the Mohawk chief continued. "There is no chance for any of you to escape. If we attack, you will be wiped out. If you surrender, your lives will be spared."

"Interesting speech," the doctor said drily. "He's probably right, too. They've had enough time to surround us."

"What are we going to do?"

"That's up to Colonel Hathorn. I'd go out and have a talk with Brant, if it were me. It might buy us some time. Brant won't want to sit around here all day. After all, some of the Lackawaxen people might have heard the shooting before, and if they did, they could guide the Warwick regiment here."

"I don't want to quit," Joel said slowly. "Even if we got back home, I wouldn't want to quit. He'd only be back."

"Amen to that," the doctor said. "But we ought to get out there and talk to him. If we could hold things up for an hour or so, we might even get a messenger through the lines to go over to the Pennsylvania side for help. They're probably not watching us as carefully now as they will be later on."

Brant's voice thundered across the cleared ground

197

again. "I warn you; you don't have a chance. Give me your pledge to return home and lay down the arms you have taken up against your King, and I will guarantee your safety until you return. You may take with you the captives from Minisink."

Colonel Hathorn strode into the center of the clearing and went over to the parapet that the men had erected down the center of the field. "Give me your attention, men!" he shouted. "What do you say to this?"

"That's a mistake," the doctor said quietly. "He's trying to foist the responsibility onto the men. And there's Meeker with him. That man has the brains of a jackass."

A chorus of catcalls came from the men at the breastwork, and Major Meeker shouted something about the brave men and the cowards.

"What shall I say?" Colonel Hathorn yelled.

"This is your only chance!" Brant thundered. "Give me your answer!"

On the edge of the clearing a musket boomed and a small cloud of dirty smoke floated from the firer's position. Brant dismounted quickly and led his horse back into the shelter of the timber.

"That's the answer!" Colonel Hathorn bawled. "We don't surrender to savages."

Joel looked at the doctor. "I guess that does it. Brant won't forget that we fired on a flag of truce."

Doctor Tusten nodded sadly. "I'm afraid it does. We needed time to save ammunition, if nothing else. And they just threw away the time like water."

"I'd better get back," Joel said. "It's going to be a long day."

"God bless you, Joel. And God save us all."

As he walked back across the clearing, he kept his head down, and he purposely zig-zagged to make a harder target. When he was halfway to the point where he had left Sturgis and Sergeant Ford, the woods around the field erupted with musketry. The sudden crash of sound reverberated from the surrounding timber and the rock outcroppings, and then he heard the drone of the heavy slugs flying almost at waist level. He bent still lower and ran for the shelter of his rifle pit and rock as hard as he could go.

He didn't feel a bit foolish.

NINETEEN

BY noon the firing had slackened. The Indians apparently didn't have too much ammunition to waste. Captain Cuddeback leaned on one elbow and kept up a running fire of conversation. Joel realized that a good deal of it was for his benefit; the captain wanted to reassure him, to make it seem as if it were simply a normal state of affairs to be sitting on top of a barren hill, surrounded by hostile Indians and Tories.

"You shoot first," the captain cautioned. "When they come, they'll come fast. You've got a rifle, so you take the long shots, and I'll hold fire and back you up. Then I'll still have a shot in my musket while you reload."

Joel nodded and swallowed.

"Ever shoot a man before?"

"No, sir."

"Well, don't worry about it. Nate Ford tells me you've got good reasons for fighting Indians."

"Yes, sir. I guess I have."

But he still wasn't sure until the first attack came. It was like the first time for anything; you never knew in advance quite how you'd act until the time came, and then you found out.

First the firing stopped and everything was quiet, except for an occasional militiaman letting off his piece at what he thought was an Indian. Then the Indians started to whoop. You still couldn't see them, but they made a noise like a pack of wolves hunting on a cold night.

The first of them came out of the timber fast, running

straight at the top of the hill. "Don't everybody go shooting at once," Sergeant Ford called anxiously. "There'll be more coming up behind these."

Joel aimed at a garishly painted brave. The front sight fell into place in the V-notch of the rear sight, and he could see a brass ornament dangling from the Indian's neck just above it. For a blinding moment he froze, while the Indian grew larger in his sights. This is a man, he thought. This is a man who is losing his land because we were too greedy. He's only fighting for what's his. And then he remembered the flames licking through the roof of the log house last fall, and the howling of the Indians as they prowled around the clearing. He squeezed the trigger, and the rifle butt kicked back against his shoulder.

"Good shooting," Captain Cuddeback said.

He rolled over and measured powder from the horn into the barrel. Patch next. Now the ball. Now the priming. Beside him, the captain's musket boomed and someone screamed. He rolled back on his stomach and sighted down the slope. There were five or six Indians still coming up the hill. They had discarded their muskets now, and they were coming on with lances and tomahawks. Joel aimed at the one nearest him and fired. The brave went down on all fours. Then he began to crawl back towards the shelter of the timber.

Joel rolled back on his side to reload. He got everything done but the priming, and then the captain yelled. He snatched his axe from his belt and dropped his rifle beside the pit and stood up. There were three of them, and they were only feet away.

Captain Cuddeback's musket boomed again, and then the captain grasped it by the barrel and swung it around his head like a club. One brave went down and another came up under the captain's arm, but Sturgis jabbed upward with a bayonet or knife, Joel couldn't see which, and the second brave fell.

And then it was over. It was quiet except for the Indians in the woods. They were chanting, now, a lugubrious wail, and the wounded on the slope were dragging themselves back out of range. Occasionally a brave darted out from the timber and hauled one of them to cover. The powder smoke lay low over the ground in a dirty haze, and the sun blazed down.

"We did a little damage," Nathan Ford said. "Maybe it'll hold them off for a while."

Joel looked back over his shoulder and his scalp prickled. Here and there men were slowly walking or crawling across the clearing to the rock ledge where Doctor Tusten had set up his hospital. Several men had been dragged to the center of the clearing, away from the firing line, and they were lying in stiff, unnatural positions. The casualties had not all been on one side.

"Do you figure they'll come back, Nate?" Captain Cuddeback asked.

"Hard to tell. If we could get Brant, they'd run like blazes. You have to get one of the big chiefs or one of the medicine men before they'll quit. I think Brant's too smart to risk getting shot. He knows they'd run away if he did."

They could see some movement in the woods. A sort of disruption of the shadows, more than anything else. A noise of breaking twigs, of murmuring voices, of wails and groans came filtering through the gloom.

"By all that's holy, I think they're pulling out," Cuddeback said. "Maybe we got a bigwig."

"Wait and see," Sturgis said.

Suddenly a voice like a trumpet came from the woods. It was Brant's voice, but he was speaking in a foreign tongue, and Joel couldn't understand him. It took him a moment before he realized that Brant was speaking Mohawk.

Sturgis crawled back out of his pit and retrieved an Indian spear that had fallen behind the perimeter. "It'll come in handy," he said. "Saves powder."

Nathan Ford looked back at him with an air of annoyance. "I want to hear what he's saying. I can make out some Mohawk."

The stentorian voice rolled in the hollow of the hills, and then there was a response, a murmuring and a swelling of voices, and then the whooping started again.

"That did it," Ford said. "He was asking them if they were all women to go running away like that. He told them if they didn't get back to fighting, he'd read them out of the tribe and send the squaws to fight instead. It kind of looks like he made his point."

The next attack was different. They came in small bunches, aimed at particular segments of the line. In front of Joel and the others in his group there was nothing to be seen, only the timber and the bright green tracery of the leaves. Somewhere on the right there was heavy firing, and the acrid smoke drifted down on them, carried by a little breeze. There was yelling, but it was as if it belonged to another world. There were screams of pain or terror, but they belonged to that other world, too.

Suddenly someone yelled, "Help us! They're breaking through!"

Captain Cuddeback leaned on his elbows. "Come on, Sturgis. Let's go give them a hand. Nate, can you and the boy hang on?"

"Sure," Sergeant Ford said. "If we need help, we'll yell."

Once Joel risked a look behind him. The Indians had come up to the parapet, and one had even got on top of it. As he watched, Cuddeback plucked him off and smashed him to the ground. There was a blur of confused motion, and then Sergeant Ford yelled, "Watch out! Here they come!"

There were six braves in line, and they ran out of the timber silently, and headed straight up the slope. Joel fired at the first one and missed. He rolled to his side and reloaded as quickly as he could. His hands were shaking, and some of the powder spilled. How long would it be before the brave he had missed would be coming over the top of the ridge, tomahawk in hand, poised for the kill?

"On your feet!" Ford snapped. His rifle cracked and Joel stood up, pulling back the hammer of his own rifle. The first brave had gone down, but the others were still coming. Now they began to yell, and Joel fired at the nearest one. The hammer snapped on an empty pan, and he realized that he had forgotten the priming. He fumbled for the powder, and then he knew it was too late, that the Indians were too close. He thrust the muzzle of the rifle forward like a lance and dodged the blow of the tomahawk at the same instant. Panic came over him like a live thing, and irrationally he wanted to break through the swarm of Indians who were being reinforced by others from the woods. He wanted to break loose and run away from the clearing where the sun beat down steadily and the acrid powder smoke hovered. He wanted to find a cool place in the woods and put his head under a cold spring until there would be nothing but the clean smell of growing things and the astringent, cleansing feel of the water. Cool water, like Susan's hands.

Light gleamed over him and he blocked the Indian's blow by grabbing his forearm. He bent the Indian's elbow backward, but the brave slithered out of his grasp.

Suddenly musketry exploded around him. He could feel the heat of the blasts and the sting of tiny grains of powder. The Indian fell backward and began rolling down the hill, and then the others began to run and stumble after him. Three of them lay dead in front of the position.

"Close," Nathan Ford said.

Captain Cuddeback nodded. "You were kind of lucky at that. I kept a weather eye out for you, and when I saw the rest of them were handling the situation back there, I took off and came back here with one of the fellows."

"Where's Sturgis?" Ford asked.

"He ain't coming back. One of them caught him before he could reload and ran a spear through his chest."

Joel heard the words as if in a dream. It was something that would have provoked wrath or sorrow on any other day. Now it was merely one incident among many.

There were no further rushes on their section of the line. Instead, the Indians maintained a steady fire from the edge of the timber, from trees, and from a rocky hill slightly to the north of the position.

'"If we can hold out until night, maybe we've got a chance," Sergeant Ford said. "They generally don't attack at night. It's bad medicine."

Cuddeback nodded gravely. "I've heard that. They figure if they get killed, they won't go to the Great Spirit. Ain't that it?"

"That's it," Ford said. "There's going to be some of us don't make it, too, for one reason or another. I'm thinking that if they get smart enough they're going to find out that they can attack from the north side of the hill. There's not much of a climb there, and the timber runs right up close. If it comes, that's where it's going to come from."

Cuddeback nodded. "I noticed earlier. If Hathorn is smart, he'll pull most of his men around to meet them and just keep a couple on the other sides."

Something moved at the edge of the timber. "Watch out," Joel said sharply. "I think they're coming back."

By now the smoke hung thick in the low spots, like a light fog. With a little breeze disturbing it from time to time, it was all but impossible to tell whether you were seeing someone moving or not. He leaned up to see, and a moment later earth and rock fragments spattered in his face, and he heard the drone of a spent ball.

"Stay down," Captain Cuddeback said. "These people ain't playing games."

A rifle cracked, and then there was the sickening thud

of a bullet striking flesh. Joel turned to see Sergeant Ford trying to get to his feet. He rolled out of his pit and went to the sergeant.

"It's my chest," Nathan Ford mumbled. Blood came from his mouth, spilling over his chin.

"Take him back to the Doc," Captain Cuddeback ordered. "I'll hold the fort here."

When he had dragged the sergeant back from the edge of the hill, he got him to his feet and over one shoulder. Ford was surprisingly heavy for a small man, and it was all he could do to carry him.

As he crossed the open space, he could hear plainly the drone of musket balls and the high-pitched pop of rifle balls overhead. The enemy was concentrating his fire on the perimeter of the hill, and the defenders were answering less actively. He was shocked to see how few of them there were.

At the rock ledge, Doctor Tusten had fourteen or fifteen men laid out, and he was moving among them with a water bottle. He had discarded his uniform coat and his sword, and his white shirt was grimy and splashed with rusty spots of dried blood.

He smiled wearily at Joel and motioned to a vacant patch of ground. "Put him down there, Joel. I'll have a look at him."

As the doctor bent over Nathan Ford, Joel looked around at the narrow patch of ground that the defenders held. All in all, there were no more than fifty men holding the hill. The key to the position seemed to be a rocky outcropping on the north side. Three men were holding the position, two of them passing loaded muskets to the third, evidently the best shot of the three.

Doctor Tusten wiped his forehead and gestured toward the three men. "If anything happens over there," he said, "we're through. We're short of ammunition, short of water, and out of food. They can walk through us any time they want to."

"How about Sergeant Ford, Doctor?"

The doctor looked tired. "He's dead, Joel. I'm sorry. He was dead when you brought him in."

He could only shake his head numbly. It was too much to comprehend all at once. Later, when there was time to think of it, there would be time to grieve, to remember that Nathan Ford had been a hard worker, that he had been a good man who was kind to him. Now there was only time to think that the position was held by three men and that it might be overrun at any moment.

"Can we hold out?" he asked the doctor.

"I don't think so," Doctor Tusten said quietly. A sudden flurry of shots drowned his next words. He smiled and spoke more loudly. "We've got five hours before it gets dark. Unless they quit now, we won't have enough ammunition to last that long."

Joel nodded. He knew without counting that he had no more than twenty or twenty-five rifle balls left. And his powder horn was suspiciously light.

"I want you to get back," the doctor was saying. "I want you to tell them what happened."

"We'll all get out, sir."

"If they carry the hill, I'm not going. I want to try to save the wounded. I think that if I can get a word with Brant, he'll listen to me. He might spare the wounded if somebody asked him to."

At any other time, Joel knew that he would have tried to persuade the doctor not to stay. But it was one thing to talk about what a person ought to do or ought not to do when you were sitting in front of a fire drinking a cup of tea; it was quite another thing when you were standing on a patch of barren ground with the sun beating down on your head and the drone of bullets around you and the reek of black powder in your nostrils. Everything except the immediate present lost meaning.

"Get back to your place, Joel," Doctor Tusten said gently.

He nodded, and then the doctor put out his hand and gripped his shoulder. "God bless you, boy."

"There's nothing much doing," Captain Cuddeback said when he came up. "I loaded Nate's rifle so I'd have two shots if they came up the hill again."

"He's dead," Joel said dully.

The captain looked at him sharply. Then he nodded as if he had expected it all along. "I liked old Nate," he said simply.

Now the firing from the woods died down to an occasional shot. The defenders were still firing to either side of them, and when he turned to look, Joel could see the three men at the rock across the clearing. As he watched, Colonel Hathorn stood up from where he had been watching the fire-fight. He made a trumpet of his hands. "Hold your fire!" he cried. "Save your ammunition!"

Captain Cuddeback grunted. "Just in case Brant didn't know we were running out of powder, Hathorn had to tell him. How they ever made him a colonel, the Almighty alone knows."

The firing slackened and died, and for almost the first time since ten o'clock in the morning, it was relatively quiet. There was only the buzz of talk, an occasional groan from the wounded. There was no sound from the woods.

"Maybe they're pulling out," Joel said hopefully.

Cuddeback shook his head. "I doubt it. Even if Brant only had eighty or ninety with him when he hit Minisink, he joined up with a lot more. I saw the place where he camped last night. He must have had better'n a hundred and fifty braves to start with this morning. Brant would never quit with that much of an edge on us."

"I don't hear anything out there."

Joel looked back across the clearing. The three men at the rock were still in position, but they had relaxed somewhat. The marksman had turned to talk to his companions, and the three of them were arguing. And then Joel stiffened. Over on the right, a single tree was moving, swaying in the breeze. But that was impossible. The other trees next to it were perfectly motionless. He was just able to make out the form of an Indian outstretched on one of the higher limbs. He wouldn't have noticed him except for the glint of metal, perhaps from his musket barrel.

Cuddeback spoke softly. "I see him. Can you reach him from here?"

"I can try. It's a far shot."

"I'll watch the front. Take a chance."

He aimed directly at the branch. Four, maybe five hundred yards. That meant he had to aim just about five feet high. He raised the muzzle, judging the distance by the trunk of the tree, and then his finger tightened on the trigger, squeezing slowly.

A tiny cloud of smoke came from the branch, and a moment later he heard the faint report of the musket. In the next instant he fired and missed.

"Too bad," Cuddeback consoled him. "If he hadn't shook your aim by firing just then, you'd probably have got him."

Suddenly the woods erupted into noise. The unearthly wolf howls of the Indians and the thudding of musketry mingled with the rustling of leaves and twigs as men poured through the underbrush. Joel risked a look at the rock. The marksman was sprawled out over it, and the other two men were grappling hand-to-hand with two braves. Joel rammed a ball home and raised his rifle.

"Watch out!" Cuddeback yelled. A tomahawk flashed by, missing his head by inches. He stood up in time to see four Indians running up the slope towards him. Cuddeback shot the first one and swung the empty musket once around his head and released it. It caught a second Indian in the chest, and he grunted and sat down. Cuddeback grabbed the rifle that had belonged to Nathan Ford, and he and Joel fired together. The other two braves went down in front of the rock.

In the center of the clearing Colonel Hathorn yelled out, "Every man for himself and God for us all!"

Cuddeback swore, and Joel reloaded automatically, burning his hand on the hot barrel of his rifle. If only he could get to the doctor! He charged into the center of the clearing only to be driven back to the edge by the snarling, clawing, clubbing mass of braves and militia, inextricably mingled. A single brave made at him and fired his musket from the hip. Pain lanced across Joel's chest, and then he stumbled over a rock and fell backwards over the edge of the hill, as the Indian clubbed the musket for a blow.

He fell over rocks that scraped and cut at his hands and knees, and then he plunged through a layer of brush and came to a stop on soft, marshy earth. He lay quiet, waiting for the Indian to follow him.

Above, the noise of firing was drowned in the screams of the dying men, the howls of the victorious braves, and he realized that the Indian wasn't going to follow him. He was too busy on top of the hill with the butchery. Joel felt of his chest and his hand came away sticky with blood. His shirt was torn in a long gash, and when he looked, he could see a furrow along one rib where the ball had grazed him. Half-an-inch further up and—never mind. The thing was, he was all right so far. He crouched and cocked his rifle. He still had a chance to get out, and there was nothing he could do for anyone on the hill. It was, as Colonel Hathorn had so aptly put it, every man for himself.

To his right was the river. It would be downhill going all the way. There might be Indians there, but it would still be safer than going overland. But he had to move fast, before they got done up on the hill.

He peered through the bushes and located another patch of brush at the base of a tree. Tensing his muscles, he burst out into the open and ran for the tree. A musket boomed off to his left, and he caught a glimpse of a pale face under a black cap ducking behind a fallen log. The face wasn't frightened. It wasn't even annoyed that it had missed its shot. It was too arrogant for that. And as he reached the illusory safety of the bushes, memory stirred, and suddenly he knew that he had found the man he had come so far to kill. Only now St. Clair was just another man. Another of the enemy.

He paused behind the tree for a moment, knowing that St. Clair would be watching to see which way he went. Still, the man had to load his piece. For a moment he would not be watching. Joel went down on all fours and crawled through the tall grass to the base of another tree off to the side of the log.

Cautiously he raised his head, and in that moment the Tory turned and saw him. He saw the musket swing towards him and the muzzle pointed at him like a silvery "O," and then the butt of his rifle slammed against his shoulder and St. Clair dropped the musket and fell forward over the log.

Automatically he swung his powder horn to the muzzle of the rifle, and then he heard the light thud of running feet in time to duck to one side. Another Tory thrust at him with a gleaming bayonet, like a splinter of ice. He knocked the musket aside with the barrel of his rifle and smashed the butt upwards into the man's chest. He ran over the Tory, not stopping to see whether he was being followed or not.

There was nothing left to do now but run.

TWENTY

HE was alert, because there was no sense in walking into a trap, but he wasn't worried about making noise, either. The thing to do was to get to the river as quickly as possible. There might be a chance to cross and find help at Lackawaxen. And even if he couldn't cross at the ford, there would be places along the bank where he could hide.

He reached the edge of the timber sobbing for breath. Even though it had been a downhill run, it had been a good mile and a half at top speed. It had paid off, though; he hadn't met a single Indian or Tory in the woods between the hill and the river. He decided that most of them had swarmed over the clearing, and that they wouldn't be pursuing the survivors who had managed to escape until they had finished taking prisoners on the hill. He hoped that Doctor Tusten had been taken prisoner.

There was a space of perhaps fifty feet of rock separating the woods from the river at the point at which he was standing. Down at the ford only a quarter of a mile away, he could see a large number of canoes drawn up on the shore. That was probably the way Brant meant to escape. Indians were moving around the canoes, evidently guarding them or getting them ready to travel. Behind him someone screamed, and the scream was followed by a series of whoops. It couldn't have come from the hill. It had to be Indians chasing one of the survivors who had tried to make it to the river.

There was only one thing to do. Get across the river as soon as he possibly could. In another ten minutes, the entire bank might be swarming with the enemy. He ran along the edge of the timber, just inside the screen of trees, until he could no longer see the ford because of a twist in the stream, and then he ran boldly across the narrow rock ledge and plunged into the river.

At first he tried to keep his rifle above water, and then he remembered that he hadn't had a chance to reload. Once he got across the river, he would be able to find a dry place where he could dry the Golcher and reload. Until then, he would just have to rely on his knife and his wits. He slung the rifle, butt uppermost.

The water was clean and fast-running and cold. It washed away the salty grime of powder smoke and the dust and blood that had clung to him, Nathan Ford's as well as his own. He waded out until the water was up to his neck, and then he spread his arms and picked up his feet and let the river carry him.

He had drifted a couple of hundred feet before they spotted him. First he heard the whoops from the bank, and then three shots boomed, echoing loudly in the river valley. He took a deep breath and dove. It was easy to stay down with the weight of the rifle to help him. He opened his eyes and saw the black, rocky bottom of the river. The rocks were covered with light green moss in places, and they looked deceptively soft. He swam with the current until his lungs ached and his vision began to blur, and then he arched his back and fought his way up the dark water until he burst into the sunlight and the life-giving air. He sucked it in greedily until he heard the hum and splash of a musket ball near him. He went down again.

Off to his right, something dark loomed up out of the river bottom. He swung over to examine it. A fallen tree that had jammed on the bottom. Good. He grasped its water-softened bark and pulled himself under it until he judged that it was between him and the Indians on the shore, and then he let himself come slowly to the surface. A few roots broke the surface of the water, and behind their screen he peered over at the opposite shore. A man was running through the shallows screaming. Behind him two braves were in hot pursuit. He didn't want to watch, but he had to anyway. Suddenly the man stumbled and fell sprawling in the water. The Indians were on him immediately.

Joel released his hold on the fallen tree and sank back against the muddy bank. The sky above him was clean and bright and blank, and he looked up at it until he thought he might escape into its brightness. He could feel himself leaving the water and the mud behind, going up into the sky, higher and higher still.

And then he knew nothing more.

It was dusk when he recovered consciousness. Everything was quiet on the opposite shore. The yelling had stopped and the gunfire. It was all over for them on the hill now. It was all over for everybody. Whoever had escaped had either made it or been caught, and there was nothing left for him to do but to get back.

He lowered himself into the water and swam with leisurely breast-strokes. It was a good way to swim, because you didn't splash and make noise the way you did otherwise. He wasn't too afraid of what lay on the other bank any more, but he was careful, anyhow.

There had been a time at the beginning of the day when he had been afraid, but he wasn't afraid now. He had been afraid of being killed, but he hadn't been. He had been afraid of running away, but he hadn't done that, either. He wasn't afraid of dying, and he wasn't afraid of living. Somehow, if he only kept his head, he was going to make it back to Goshen, and then the rest would take care of itself.

When he was half-a-mile down from the fallen tree, he edged out into the middle of the stream and let the current take him down until he saw a point of land jutting out from the northern shore. Then he started to swim again until he could touch bottom, and then he waded ashore. There was no sound from the timber, and he moved into it quickly, so that he would not be silhouetted against the water, which was bright with the last light of day. He moved well inside the timber and squatted down in a clump of bushes and unslung his rifle.

The lock of the Golcher was well-oiled, and if any water had got into it, it would soon run out through the trigger slot. The barrel would be wet, though, and the pan. He wiped off the pan with his hand and blew on it. Then he blew through the touchhole into the barrel. And then he waited.

When it was almost dark, he took one of the oiled patches from the patch box in the butt and rammed it down the barrel. With the worm attached to the ramrod, he withdrew it and held it against his cheek. It was dry. He loaded the rifle then, first blowing on the exposed parts once more, just to make sure that they were dry and wouldn't dampen the charge. He was ready to travel.

He headed out of the river valley, and a surprising thing happened. As he began the climb that would put him on top of Shawangunk, the day seemed to return. Down in the valley along the river it was already dark, but here on the slope of the mountain it was light enough to see fifty or sixty yards ahead of him in the bare places. He would be able to keep going until it got black dark, and then he would rest until the stars gave him enough light to see by. If you waited long enough, no matter how black the night was, the stars would always come out, or the day would come.

Maybe that was true of everything you did, not only of walking at night. The important thing wasn't doing everything at once. It was doing what you could do when you had to do it. And never giving up.

He slept on the flank of Shawangunk that night, about five miles below Minisink, and about the same distance from

216

the claim. His side hurt him because he had nothing to tie around the wound to keep his shirt from rubbing against it. It was cold enough so that he could have used a fire, but he was too tired to draw the charge from his rifle so that he could start one, and besides there was always the chance that some of Brant's men might be roaming around trying to pick up small groups of survivors.

He slept fitfully, and when it got light enough to see he moved out towards the fold in the hills where Goshen lay. About six miles from the Tusten house he struck the trail he and Adam had used last winter, and he followed that until he came in sight of the house. He didn't pay too much attention to the trail. He had a lot of thinking to do, and his side hurt as if someone had stuck a knife in it. When he looked under his shirt, the flesh was laid back and crusted over with blood. Where the crust didn't hide it, it was black and blue.

It was a funny thing, but his side hadn't hurt nearly so much yesterday. Even last night it hadn't been as bad as it was now. He guessed that it was because he had had a lot of other things on his mind like swimming the river two ways and running away from the Indians and keeping out of sight. Now that he didn't have to worry about it so much, he had more time to think about how his side hurt.

Then he looked at the house, white and solid and permanent in the sun, and he thought about walking up to the door and seeing them smiling, waiting for the doctor to come. They would all greet him, the children too, and then they would ask when the doctor would be back, and then he would have to tell them. It would be easier to fight yesterday all over again than it would be to tell them that the doctor wasn't coming back.

He thought about it for a moment, and then he knew that it was something he was going to have to do, just like he had had to go to the battle.

He walked around to the back door. Captain Cuddeback was standing at the well curb, washing himself out of a tin basin. He stared at Joel as if he had seen a ghost.

"I didn't think anybody else got away," he said. And then he reached out and grabbed Joel's hand. "I'm awful glad to see you, Joel," he said simply.

"Did the doctor make it out?"

Cuddeback winced and shook his head. "Hathorn made it and maybe about a dozen more, but the Doc never had a chance. I was about the last one out and they were all over the place. I saw them get to where the Doc was, and all I could see then was Indians and more Indians. He never had a chance."

Joel nodded. Somehow he had expected it. "I was afraid of that. I tried to get to him, but I got chased." He looked towards the house. "Do they know in there?"

Cuddeback nodded. "I told them. I guess I was about the first one back. I stopped over to home, and then I come here." He looked suddenly angry. "The first one, that is, except for the men who couldn't keep up and sat on their tails back in a swamp while the rest of us were up on that hill fighting."

It didn't bother him a lot, what the others had done or hadn't done. He had done what he had to do. That was what counted.

"They asked about you," Cuddeback said, nodding towards the house. "I said I didn't know."

"All right. I'll go tell them I'm here."

He wasn't worried any more. Once you found out what you could do and what you couldn't do, you had crossed the line that separated a boy from a man. Yesterday he had crossed the line, and he would never have to worry about it again. Somehow the doctor had prepared him for it by his teaching and by his example, so that when the time came to be a man, he had been ready. It left him owing the doctor a debt, and it was the kind of debt you could only pay in one way.

Someone had to take the place of the man who had died for the thing he had believed in most: the right of the sick and the infirm to have a chance to live. Someone had to take his place. A man who could set aside his personal desires when they conflicted with his responsibilities. A man who could not only stand on his own feet, but who could help others stand on theirs. Maybe he could be that man. He had to try.

Maybe he still could become a doctor. He wanted to badly enough. But that wasn't the important thing. The important thing right now was to take care of the shop that had been Nathan Ford's so that Mrs. Ford would have a living. It was to try to help Mrs. Tusten run the farm for as long as she needed him.

It was a funny thing, but he felt almost as if the doctor were standing beside him now, pointing out the things that had to be done, showing him how to do them. He suddenly realized that there would never be a time when he would not be conscious of the doctor standing beside him.

He turned towards the kitchen door, and just then Susan came out. The sun glinted on her hair and the sheen of her skin. Joel thought that she had never looked so lovely before. She ran to meet him.

AUTHOR'S NOTE

Although this is an historical novel, several of the characters were actual persons. The Tusten family was real as were Joseph Brant, Colonel Hathorn, Captain Cuddeback, Major Meeker, and Major Decker. Other than these, the characters are imaginary.

The best life of Doctor Benjamin Tusten is to be found in a pamphlet prepared by the Tusten Centennial Committee, *Tusten Centennial, July 26 to August 1, 1953*. This is quoted from Samuel Eager's *History of Orange County*, which is apparently the source for all information on Doctor Tusten.

The town of Minisink no longer exists. It was located about six miles northeast of the present city of Port Jervis, on the east bank of the small creek that feeds the Neversink River. The settlement of Big Eddy, at the bend in the Delaware, was located at the site of Port Jervis. Lackawaxen and Goshen are still very much in evidence, and they can be located on any good New York State map.

Charles Stickney, in his *A History of the Minisink Region*, indicates that the raid on Minisink occurred at dawn on July 20. Since the news was not received by Lieutenant Colonel Tusten until the evening of the twentieth, I feel that the raid may have occurred later in the day than Stickney indicates.

The battle of Minisink occured July 22, 1779. Perhaps

the best account of the battle is to be found in William Leete Stone's *The Life of Joseph Brant*. Other accounts are in Ruttenber's *History of Orange County, N. Y.*, and in Twichell's *History of the Minisink Country*, which contains the report of Colonel Hathorn, made several days after the battle. The report is an attempt to explain the defeat to Governor Clinton, and minimizes the bad judgement of Hathorn and of Major Meeker. It is fairly obvious that Brant's force was augmented by reserves before the battle; an American observer on the day following observed Brant's retreat up the Delaware and estimated his force to be considerably larger than the ninety odd men who raided Minisink.

The Minisink battleground is located near Lackawaxen, on the north side of the Delaware. It is still possible to see Doctor Tusten's hospital rock and to trace the battle lines of that hot July day when the Goshen Regiment stood and slugged it out with a superior force in order that their community might be spared the fate of Minisink.

There were some few prisoners taken by Brant after the battle. Curiously enough, Colonel Hathorn gave orders before the battle that no quarter was to be shown Brant's men. Brant, on the other hand, was willing to accept surrender until he was fired on while under the flag of truce. The musket ball passed through his sword belt and did no physical injury, but the incident was doubtless rankling enough to cause Brant to overlook his first impulse of mercy.

Some forty years after the battle, the bones of the fallen were collected for burial. One skeleton lay somewhat apart from the hospital rock and had been laid in a rock cairn. The limbs were straightened, and remnants of a Continental uniform were still in evidence. A legend grew to the effect that Joseph Brant in this manner had honored some gallant enemy whose conduct in action had been extremely praiseworthy. Twichell cites the incident and the legend in his *History of the Minisink Country*, and believes that the soldier so honored was Benjamin Tusten. So do I.

222

SOURCES

Carmer, Carl. *The Susquehanna*. New York, 1955.

Eager, Samuel H. *A History of Orange County*. Newburgh, N.Y., 1847.

Ruttenber, E. M. *History of Orange County, New York*. Newburgh, N.Y., 1875.

Seese, Mildred Parker. *Old Orange Homes*. 2 vols. Middletown, N.Y., 1941–43.

Stickney, Charles E. *A History of the Minisink Region*. Middletown, N.Y., 1867.

Stone, William Leete. *The Life of Joseph Brant*. 2 vols. New York, 1838.

Tusten Centennial Committee. *Tusten Centennial, July 26 to August 1, 1953*. 1953.

Twitchell, Horace E. *History of the Minisink Country*. Port Jervis, N.Y., 1912.

Ray Grant Toepfer was born in Hays, Kansas, and attended school in Gorham, Kansas. He later attended the University of Wisconsin and received a master's degree in English literature from the university before entering the army in World War II.

During his military service he was stationed in Greenland, serving as librarian and as editor of the base newspaper. Following his discharge, he was married and worked for a time as an advertising copywriter and encyclopedia editor.

His first novel, *The Scarlet Guidon,* was published in 1958 and was described by *The Library Journal* as "a vivid and readable portrayal of the War on the Southern side."

In 1963 he enrolled in the Ph.D. program of the City University of New York, at Hunter College, and he is currently working on his doctorate. In addition to his studies and his writing, he teaches English and creative writing at Brooklyn College.

Mr. Toepfer's wife and two teenage daughters all take an active interest in his writing career. He and his family live in New York City.